Revolting Stories
For Nine Year Olds

Helen Paiba is known as one of the most committed, knowledgeable and acclaimed children's booksellers in Britain. For more than twenty years she owned and ran the Children's Bookshop in Muswell Hill, London, which under her guidance gained a superb reputation for its range of children's books and for the advice available to its customers.

Helen was involved with the Booksellers Association for many years and served on both its Children's Bookselling Group and the Trade Practices Committee. In 1995 she was given honorary life membership of the Booksellers Association of Great Britain and Ireland in recognition of her outstanding services to the association and to the book trade. In the same year the Children's Book Circle (sponsored by Books for Children) honoured her with the Eleanor Farjeon Award, given for distinguished service to the world of children's boo~~

She retired in 1995 and ~

D1506601

Revolting

STORIES

For Nine Year Olds

COMPILED BY HELEN PAIBA

ILLUSTRATED BY JUDY BROWN

MACMILLAN
CHILDREN'S BOOKS

First published 2001 by Macmillan Children's Books
a division of Pan Macmillan Limited
20 New Wharf Road, London N1 9RR
Basingstoke and Oxford
www.panmacmillan.com

Associated companies throughout the world

ISBN 0 330 48370 6

3 5 7 9 8 6 4 2

A CIP catalogue record for this book is available from the
British Library.

Typeset by SX Composing DTP, Rayleigh, Essex
Printed and bound in Great Britain by
Mackays of Chatham plc, Kent

Contents

Piddler on the Roof

Paul Jennings

Dad and I were having a pee in the garden. Dad stood there staring at the moon and listening to the soft splash of wee on the grass. "Poetry," he said. "It's the only word for taking a leak in your own backyard."

I unzipped my fly. "Magic," I said.

Mum thought it was disgusting but there was nothing she could do about it. Dad said that Man had been standing in the forest peeing on the plants since the dawn of time. He had a speech all worked out about nature and Ancient Man sitting around the campfire.

"It's only natural," he would say, "for a man to get out and watch the stars . . ."

"Twinkle," I would yell.

Then we would both start to laugh like crazy. Every time it was the same old joke about the stars

1

twinkling but we always thought it was funny. My dad was a great bloke. And we were great mates.

So there we were, standing side by side. Watering the lawn.

"Swordfight," I yelled.

"You're on, sport," said Dad.

Our two streams of pee crossed each other in the darkness like two watery blades fighting it out in times of old. Usually I ran out of ammo first and Dad would win. But tonight I beat him easily.

"Well done, Weesle," said Dad. "You're amazing. You could beat a horse."

I blushed with pride and grinned as we walked back to the house. I remembered the time when the kids at school treated me like a little squirt. But that was long ago, before I proved myself in the great peeing competition.

Now life was really good.

But not for long.

"Look at this," said Mum. Her eyes were glued to the television as she spoke. "The tap water has got bugs in it. It's been contaminated. No one in the whole of Sydney can drink our water."

"We'll have to drink Coke," I said hopefully.

"Bottled water," said Mum. "They're selling it

2

in all the shops."

"We won't be able to have a shower," I said even more hopefully.

"You can wash in it," said Mum. "But not drink it. It's disgraceful."

We stood there listening to the man on the news saying how it was dangerous to drink the water. Especially for old people.

And children.

When he said the last two words I sort of felt funny inside. Mum and Dad were staring at me with a strange look in their eyes.

"Oh, no," I yelled. "No, you don't. I'm not leaving. I'm not going back to the Outlaws."

"You know what the doctor told you," said Dad. "One more infection and you're gone."

I smacked my fist into my palm angrily. It was true. I had a problem with my lungs. If I got infected it was serious.

"Not the Outlaws," I said. "Please."

"I wish you wouldn't call my sister and Ralph 'the Outlaws'," said Mum.

"Dad does," I started to say. He was shaking his head at me. He didn't want me to dob him in. He was the one who started calling Aunty Sue and Ralph the Outlaws. He couldn't stand them either.

3

"Sorry, mate," said Dad. "But you'll have to go to Dingle until the scare is over."

I stared hopelessly at them both. I decided to save my breath. When they both lined up against me there was no way I could win.

The next morning I stepped off the train at Dingle. Horrible Aunty Sue and her even more horrible son, Ralph, were there to meet me.

"Hello, Weesle," said Ralph in a sickly sweet voice. "I'm looking forward to this."

He was too, and I knew why.

"Get in the car, Weesle," said Aunty Sue. "We're running late. This visit really is inconvenient. You couldn't have come at a worse time. You'll have to look after yourself. I'm too busy with the hospital fête."

"I'll look after him again," said Ralph with a sneer.

Aunty Sue smiled at him. "You are a kind boy," she said. She picked up my bag and frowned.

"What have you got in here?" she said.

"Bottled water," I told her.

"You don't need that here, droob," said Ralph. "Our water is pure. Not like the stinky stuff in the city."

4

"The doctor said I have to," I told him. "Just to be on the safe side. But I'm allowed to drink lemonade."

"No soft drinks," snapped Aunty Sue. "Bad for your teeth."

I secretly felt the ten dollars in my pocket. I could buy my own Coke.

Aunty Sue and Ralph lived in a small cottage in the middle of Dingle. My room was up in the roof.

I plonked down my bags and sat on the bed. Ralph closed the door so Aunty Sue couldn't hear. He held out his hand. "Pay up, Weesle," he said. "A dollar a day. Pay the rent."

Ralph was much bigger than me. And he was a bully. But I shook my head.

"No way," I said. "Not this time. You can sneak on me all you like. Last time I stayed ten days. Ten dollars. All my pocket money. I need it to buy Coke. I can't just drink water the whole time."

Ralph stood up and left. He didn't say a word. He didn't have to. We both knew what he was going to do.

Dob. Rat on me. Tell tales.

Call it what you like. It is the same thing. He was going to tell Aunty Sue every time I did the slightest thing wrong.

And he did. Right away.

Aunty Sue held out her hand. "Give me the ten dollars, Weesle," she said. "Soft drinks are bad for your teeth."

I handed over the ten dollars with a big sigh. This was going to be a long ten days.

The way it turned out it was a long ten hours. Ralph dobbed me in for the smallest little thing.

"Mum, Weesle didn't wipe his feet."

"Inconsiderate child," said Aunty Sue.

"Mum, Weesle didn't clean his teeth."

"Unhealthy child," said Aunty Sue.

"Mum, Weesle stole some ice cream."

"Thief," yelled Aunty Sue.

"Mum, Weesle picked his nose."

"Disgusting child," sniffed Aunty Sue.

"Mum, Weesle didn't wash his hands before the meal."

"Filthy boy," yelled Aunty Sue.

This went on all afternoon. Aunty Sue had a thing about health. You had to have clean fingernails. You had to wipe your mouth with a napkin after a meal. You had to spray stuff that smelled of flowers around the toilet. You had to search the plug-hole in the shower for hairs after you had used it.

Aunty Sue was a health freak of the worst sort. And every time I broke a rule Ralph would dob on me.

By the time night came I just couldn't take any more. I looked out of my little attic window on the roof and blinked back tears. I wanted to go home. I wanted to see Mum again. I wanted Dad. I wanted my own messy room.

I looked up at the stars.

I wanted a twinkle.

I was really busting by the time I got outside. Oh, it was lovely to be out there in the backyard at night. It reminded me of Dad and our swordfights. And our conversations about the meaning of life.

I quickly pulled down my fly and let fly.

"Filthy, disgusting, despicable child." The words broke the peaceful night like a stone thrown through a window. It was Aunty Sue. And Ralph. He had dobbed on me. He knew I liked to take a leak in the garden. And he had told Aunty Sue.

"Get back inside," she shrieked. "Get back to your room. And don't leave it. Stay in that room and don't come out. Weesle, you are disgusting. You're going home first thing in the morning."

I couldn't see Ralph's face. But I knew it had a smirk plastered all over it.

It was agony trying to stop the pee. Trying to stop in mid-piddle is really bad for your health. It is just torture. But I used all of my strength and managed to stop the flow. I pulled up my zip, raced back up to my room and slammed the door.

There was good news and bad news.

The good news was that they were sending me home in the morning. Terrific.

The bad news was that I couldn't leave the room to go to the loo. And I was busting to finish my leak.

There is really nothing worse than needing to

have a pee and not being able to.

I knew that if I left the room Ralph would dob.

The minutes ticked by. Then the hours. The pressure built up. The pain was terrible. Unbearable. I rolled around on the bed. I staggered around the room with my knees held together. Finally, I couldn't stand it any longer. I ran to the little attic window and threw it open.

Oh, wonderful, wonderful, wonderful. The yellow stream fizzled out into the night like a burst water main. A beautiful melody. Magic. Music to the ear. Wee on a tin roof is not as good as wee on the grass. But it is still a lovely sound. I smiled as it splashed on the metal and trickled down into the spouting.

The next morning Aunty Sue pushed me on to the train. "Go back to the filthy city and its filthy water," she said.

"Yeah," said Ralph. "Our tank water is pure."

"Is it?" I said.

The Curse of Dogbreath Magroo

Colin Thompson

At the back of the house up its own narrow staircase was the room of Dogbreath Magroo. It was a cold dim room known to the rest of the house as the Two-Day Room because that was the longest anyone had ever stayed there. Most people went the next morning. Some didn't even unpack their suitcases, they just turned around and left straight away.

Shadows gathered in the corners of the room, shadows that shivered and fidgeted as they tried to hide behind each other. At the one thin window was a torn grey rag, a shadow too of a once bright curtain covered in roses. The roses were echoed on the walls and like the curtain they had faded and died. The air was clammy and thick and green.

Dogbreath Magroo had been an old sea dog who lived in the room when he came back from the ocean. All his life he had travelled the oceans of the world and in every harbour and every inn the name of Dogbreath Magroo had left the same memory, a memory that could cause grown men to weep and women to faint clean away. Dogbreath Magroo had had the breath of a twenty-year-old dog that had eaten rotten cabbage leaves all his life. And this was hardly surprising because he *was* a twenty-year-old dog and he *had* eaten rotten cabbage leaves all his life.

He had lived in this room and he had died there. He had lain dead there for weeks before anyone had noticed. When something dies, after a while it begins to smell, but Dogbreath Magroo did that anyway. It was only when he stopped smelling so bad that they knew he was dead.

They had to hold auditions to find someone who could carry the old dog into the garden and bury him. Having no sense of smell just wasn't enough, for the smell of Dogbreath Magroo was so powerful you could hear it and you could feel it on your skin. At last they found someone for the job. They found someone who could sit in a bath of rancid goat yoghurt with pieces of hundred-year-old French cheese dribbling from each nostril while eating a third-hand handkerchief. They found someone with no sense of hearing, sight or smell who could feel his way into the room and fetch the old dog, someone who would do anything if the price was right.

"We should have thought of asking our accountant before," said Peter's dad. "It would have saved a lot of trouble."

By the time Dogbreath Magroo was taken out of the room, his smell had left him and become a ghost. It had crept into every crack between the floorboards and behind every wrinkle in the wallpaper. It had grown and multiplied until it had taken over the whole room. The smell hid and mutated and even pretended not to be there by disguising itself as a lovely vase of flowers.

There was a never-ending line of tenants willing to rent the room. It had a lovely view as the house was in a beautiful spot right on the water. The lodgers just couldn't believe how cheap it was. But it was the same every time. They dragged their suitcase bumping up the narrow staircase, hung their clothes in the wardrobe, put the framed photo of their mum on the chest of drawers and lay down for a snooze.

During the day, the ghost of Dogbreath Magroo lay still and waited. To get the full force of its powers it needed darkness. A bit of moonlight was even better. Then, while the unsuspecting visitor slept, it would do its evil. Everything in the room, even down to the mother's photograph, was soon filled with the terrible smell.

And with the smell came the hair. Everything was buried under a thick layer of dog hair. Beautiful smart black suits and thick woollen sweaters were ruined for ever. The hairs were rooted deep into the clothes so no amount of brushing or cleaning could ever remove them, and whatever colour the clothes were, the hair was the opposite. The ghost could even cover the most complicated tartan with hair in six different colours. Of course, the smell was so terrible that most people didn't even notice the hair until they had packed and fled.

It was the same every time. Peter's mum had never managed to get anyone to stay in the room for more than two nights and then they had to be very drunk. They tried to remove the ghost with the exorcise bike but because it was a dog, it chased the wheels and bit the tyres.

"Something's got to be done," she said. "We need the money."

"It'll end in tears," said Peter's granny.

"We need an exorcist," said Peter's dad, "to drive the ghost away."

"Well, you'd better get a good one," said Peter's granny. "We don't want it turning up somewhere else in the house."

There wasn't anything in the *Yellow Pages* or on the noticeboard at the sweet shop. They advertised for someone and two or three people came, but none of them was any good. They swept in wearing shiny black cloaks, velvet top hats and crept out covered in clouds of white dog hairs and confusion.

"We have to be more specific," said Peter's mum. "We have to say exactly what the ghost is. We need a specialist."

"I shouldn't think there's an exorcist that just gets rid of dog ghosts," said Peter's dad.

But there was.

A week later there was a ring at the door and a little old lady stood there. Her lumpy cardigan was done up on the wrong buttons and her tweed skirt was already covered in dog hairs.

"I've come about the advert," she said. "I am Gertrude Pencil and I have come to exercise the ghost of your dog."

"Don't you mean exorcise?" said Peter's mum.

"I know what I mean," said Gertrude Pencil.

"Can I watch?" asked Alice.

"You can get me a nice cup of tea with three sugars and a biscuit," said Gertrude. She went into the bathroom, sat on the bed and started chanting in a strange foreign language.

"Leeh, leeh," she wailed, then, "slurp, slurp," as she drank her tea uttering a strange curse as her biscuit broke and fell in the cup.

All afternoon she sat cross-legged on the bed chanting. Alice sat in an old armchair and watched and at half-past four, the shape of Dogbreath Magroo appeared in the middle of the floor. It was faint at first but as the old lady reached out towards it, it became more solid and wagged its tail. The smell was terrible but the old lady didn't seem to notice.

"Leeh, leeh," she wailed, "leeh, leeh."

The ghost of Dogbreath Magroo walked over to the bed and the old lady reached down and stroked it.

"Seiklaw," she muttered and the dog followed

her downstairs and out of the house never to be seen again. And only Alice knew the secret of the strange language for only she had been listening in a mirror.

Van Gogh's Potatoes

Mary Arrigan

For as far back as I could remember I always looked forward to the last week in August. That's when I'd be dropped off at Gran's old red-brick house that stood in its own grounds behind a high wall. My pals slagged me.

"Staying with an old fossil like that in a big, gloomy house? You're daft."

But they didn't know my gran. They didn't know how much we laughed together. That summer, when I was ten, she moved me from my usual cosy back room with its sloping ceiling and sunny walls into a big, sombre room at the end of the corridor. A room that, no matter how it tried, the sun would never fill with light.

"You're a big lad now, Vince," she said. "You need a big room."

I looked around. With its high ceiling and acres

18

of frayed carpet, it was much too big for me. All that space would swallow me up. I hated it. And I hated the ugly furniture that loomed in the eerie darkness. How could I tell Gran that I preferred the boy-friendly clutter of the old room? She was beaming at me.

"I had it papered only last week," she said. "Just for you."

I swallowed. You'd hardly notice the yellow wallpaper, lost in the shadows, which made the room seem even sadder. That was it. That was the main feeling that came from these walls – sadness. However, there was no point in disappointing the old lady.

"Great," I croaked. "Just great, Gran."

I put off going to bed for as long as I possibly could. We played game after game of Scrabble for high stakes and fought loudly over iffy words. Finally Gran yawned.

"Go on up to bed, lad," she said, "before we both fall down in a heap from exhaustion."

There was no putting off the moment any longer. I shuffled along the dark corridor and eased myself into that room.

Sleep was slow to visit me that night. In spite of leaving the light on, the gloomy shadows seemed full of a sadness that was trying to pull me in. I sat up and pulled the duvet around my chin. It was then that I noticed the two pictures above my bed. Both of them were painted in dark colours that emphasized the dreary subjects. The one on the right showed a group of five people dressed in heavy, old-fashioned peasant clothes. They were sitting around a table in the light of a hanging lamp. Except for the person in the foreground, who had her back to me, the others were extremely ugly. A man with a cap was offering some food to a sour-faced old bat who was pouring something into cups. A younger woman, who was about to put a fork into some food, was facing outwards. She was wearing a ridiculous floppy bonnet. Her bulging eyes were looking directly at me, as if I hadn't enough to freak me out in this crummy room. I looked away from her scary gaze. Why anyone would want to paint a picture like that and hang it on a wall was way beyond me.

But it was the other picture that really stirred up my jittery nerves. Talk about gloom and doom! It was a small black and white print which showed a boy and a girl about my own age. They were stick-thin, scrabbling in what looked like stony ground. Their haunted, starved eyes were looking

directly at me, as if pleading with me to help them. Behind them was a crude hovel, its door open to show a bundle of rags just inside. We'd learned all about the Irish famine at school, so I knew what was going on. That was a disaster that happened in the 1840s when the potato crop failed and thousands of people starved to death. Did those children know that I was sitting here, with my fishfingers and chips supper inside me, looking at their misery?

Even after I turned out the light and covered my head, the hungry eyes of the kids and the bulging eyes of the ugly woman burned right through to mess up my head. Again there was that sense of being pulled towards something unknown. I clung to the duvet and fought off the urge to yell for Gran. Tomorrow I'd definitely ask her to let me move back to my old room. When sleep finally caught up with my racing mind, I dreamed a jumble of frightening dreams, so real that I woke up in a sweat. Mostly they were dreams about eyes and hunger. And cries. People crying out in hunger and I could do nothing to help them.

When Gran came in to call me the next morning, I felt like I'd been chewed up and spat out by some mega-monster. "Those pictures, Gran," I said, pointing without actually looking at them in case those eyes would catch me.

"What about them?" she asked as she pulled back the curtain to let in a pathetic sunbeam that only emphasized the gloom in the rest of the room.

"They're scary," I said.

"Scary?" said Gran. She came over and leaned towards the two pictures. "No. Not scary. That one," she said, pointing to the ugly munchers, "is called *The Potato Eaters*. It was painted by a man called Van Gogh. Vincent Van Gogh." She looked at me and smiled. "Same name as yourself." She looked back at the picture. "This is a print. The original is in the Van Gogh Museum in Amsterdam."

"Huh," I said. "Can't say I'm thrilled to share a name with a man who paints clumsy clods like that. Look at them, they're horrible."

Gran peered closer. She shook her head. "No they're not," she murmured. "They have a beauty all their own. They're ordinary people doing ordinary things. Beauty is not about pretty faces, Vince. It's to do with what's inside. It's to do with loving and sharing and—"

"Yeah, sure, Gran," I put in. "But they're still dead ugly. What about the other picture? Where's the beauty in that?"

Gran nodded. "No beauty there," she admitted. "That's an engraving showing the hunger during—"

"During the famine," I interrupted again. "I know that. But don't you think it's a bit gross? Who wants to look at that sort of thing? I wish you'd take them away. Or else I wish I could go back to my old room."

Gran threw my clothes at me and laughed. "You mean you're afraid of a couple of pictures? And there was I thinking that you'd grown up. Ha!"

We didn't mention the pictures or the room

again that day. We went for a drive in Gran's clapped-out old Ford Fiesta and had some nosh in a Kentucky Fried Chicken place. It wasn't until we came out into the night after seeing a movie that I remembered that awful, sad room with its awful, sad pictures.

"Gran," I said as we closed the garage doors, "about my old room . . ."

"Oh, shoot!" she said. "I forgot. I put a whole lot of junk in there when I had the decorators in. And the bed is not made up."

"That doesn't matter," I put in. "I can just take the sheets off the bed I slept in last night."

But she was shaking her head. "When I say it's not made up I mean it's been dismantled. They took it apart to make room for all the stuff. Look, can't you just sleep where you are for tonight? Tomorrow we'll put the old bed together again and you can move back, all right?"

I nodded. Suddenly the day's fun crumbled as the thoughts of another night in that great tomb of a bedroom took over. And those cruddy pictures.

"Shall I take out the pictures?" asked Gran, as if she'd read my mind. "You were saying you thought they were creepy."

"The pictures?" I forced a laugh, like the brave

24

lad I was. "Don't be daft. They're only bits of paper in frames, Gran. What do you think I am? Some sort of scaredy cat?"

Which is exactly what I was, but I certainly wasn't going to have my gran think so. Not now that I was ten.

There are only so many times you can wash your hands without them turning white and puckered, but that night I didn't care if I scrubbed through to the bones as long as it delayed going to bed. Gran had turned on the lamp and even put a hot-water bottle in my bed, but that did nothing to cheer the sad room. There even seemed to be an extra chill that crept under my skin. I stole a glance at all the eyes. Yes, there they were, devouring me. I dived under the duvet, but it didn't shut out the fear that filled my throat.

Coming up for air was about the worst decision I ever made. Where the lamp had been, a spluttering candle gave out a feeble spark against a cold dawn. Through an open doorway two figures were silently scrabbling in the stony earth. What was going on here? Before I could cry out, one of the figures outside turned towards me. Hungry eyes that were all too familiar stared in my direction. There was that pulling sensation again and I tried to shrink away from those eyes, to fight against whatever was drawing me into this scene.

"Give us a hand here," she said. "There must be something left."

Hold on a sec, I tried to cry out, but my voice was lost in a fog of fear. What was I doing here? I didn't like this dream. I wanted out. But the sharp dawn air was too real for a dream. In a puzzled, frightened daze I went towards the doorway. The bleak landscape outside stretched for miles. Now the boy turned.

"Don't lie down again," he croaked. "Help us to dig."

Don't bother, I tried to say. *There's no point. The potatoes are all rotten. There's nothing in the ground.* But the words wouldn't come. It was then I realized that the children were not looking at me at all. Their words were for the skeletal figure that was emerging from a bundle of rags. It was a woman with a small child in her arms. She dragged herself towards the children and added her weak efforts to theirs.

"We'll find something to eat, Ma," said the boy, panting with effort. "You'll see."

But the gaunt woman was shaking her head. "Our only hope is to get to a soup kitchen," she said. "If we could just have some hot soup, we'd be able to make the journey to the city. There's help in the city."

Don't be daft! I tried to shout. *The cities are overflowing. People are dropping dead from disease and starvation. You haven't a hope.* But, once more, the words didn't come.

The girl stood up, put her hands on her bony hips and looked at her mother.

"Ma," she said. "We'd never make it to the soup kitchen, never mind the city. We're stuck here. We can go no further. At least we have shelter from the rain."

The mother sank to her knees. "It's hopeless," she said. "It's just so hopeless." The three of them looked at one another with a look that it didn't take a genius to work out. They saw death in each other's faces and knew they could do nothing about it.

I'll help! I tried to shout. I forced myself closer to these skinny, ragged people, all fear gone as I struggled desperately to tell them I wanted to help them. But I found myself being pulled away. The mother was shuffling back into the hovel. I tried to get back to them, but the pull brought me farther away. I realized I was looking at the scene on the print above the bed.

"*I'll help!*" I screamed. This time my voice rang out. The two children turned towards me, their eyes looking straight into mine. "*I'll help you,*" I cried again, wondering why my legs wouldn't take me back to those desperate people. Why was the scene getting swallowed up in fog? I was shouting with frustration.

"Why such a fuss?"

At first I couldn't see the person behind the voice. The air was different. It was warm and it smelled of cooking and logs burning. A strangely comforting smell in this awful place. Place? What place? The fog was all around me. "What's all the fuss?" the voice asked again. The crude face of the woman with the floppy bonnet was looking directly at me, just like in the picture by the man with my name. I looked around for her eating companions, but she was standing alone in the mist. Funny, those eyes that had scared me mindless didn't frighten me, now that my fear was for that starving family.

"I'm Gordina," she said, coming closer to me. I could see the folds in her dress and the stitching in her bonnet. "Gordina De Groot. I'm Mister Van Gogh's favourite model. Tell me what's troubling you, boy."

I told her about the family I'd just left and about my desperate need to help them.

"What can I do?" I said when I'd finished.

She touched me with her calloused, peasant hands and smiled. And, as she looked at me, I saw beyond the thick lips and big nose. I saw the kindness and love, the beauty that Gran had spoken of.

"Don't worry," she said. "Wait and look." Her hand slipped away and the mist got thicker.

"*Wait!*" I called out. "What do you mean?" But she was gone.

"What are you shouting about? Poor lad, I should have known that second helping of chicken nuggets would give you nightmares."

I gasped as Gran pulled the duvet from my head. I looked frantically around for Gordina and the starving children. But there was just the cool dawn light in my room. Gran smiled and smoothed my forehead. "There, there," she said. Whatever "there there" was supposed to do for someone in a blind panic, but she meant well in a granny sort of way. I lay back, exhausted, on my pillow.

"Bad dream," I muttered.

Gran nodded. "Lie-in in the morning," she said.

"I'll bring you a rasher and egg on a tray. How about that?"

As she got up, she glanced at the pictures. "How odd," she mused.

"What do you mean?" I sat bolt upright. *Please, not more weird stuff.*

Gran leaned closer to the pictures. "Something's different."

I knelt on the bed and looked, fearful of what I might see. Gordina De Groot's eyes stared back at me, with just the smallest indication of a smile. And the potatoes. Was it my imagination or were there now fewer potatoes in *The Potato Eaters*? Then I looked at the famine print. The two children were still looking at me. But that hungry look had been replaced by a contented expression. On the ground where they'd scrabbled for food, there were now several fat potatoes.

Godfrey's Revenge

Dick King-Smith

"Mummy," said Godfrey. "Where's Daddy?"

"Why do you ask?" said Godfrey's mother.

"Because I haven't seen him lately," said Godfrey.

"When did you last see your father?"

"Just before Christmas. What's happened to him?"

"Godfrey," said his mother, "I'm afraid your daddy is dead."

"Dead?" cried Godfrey. "How did he die?"

"He had his head chopped off with an axe."

"But why?"

"Oh, stop your endless questions, do!" snapped his mother, and she strutted off to the henhouse to lay an egg.

Godfrey was an unusual chicken. His brothers and sisters ran about the farmyard, pecking and

31

scratching and cheeping and flapping, all in a thoughtless way.

But Godfrey was curious about the world into which he had been hatched. He wanted to know why birds like sparrows or starlings or crows flew in the sky while chickens couldn't. He wanted to know why the farmer and his family all wore clothes while the animals didn't. He wanted to know why the sun was hot and the rain wet.

Godfrey was for ever asking questions. And the question now was – why had his father been killed? Who should he ask? His mother had snapped at him. His brothers and sisters, and for that matter all the other chickens, were, in his opinion, feather-brained.

Deep in thought, Godfrey pottered off down the farmyard. As he reached the pigsties, he saw that in one of them a pig was staring out at him, resting its front trotters on the sty wall. Godfrey looked up at it.

"Excuse me," he said politely. "I wonder if you can help me?" The pig grunted.

Is that a yes or a no? thought Godfrey. He tried again.

"You see," he said, "my father has been murdered."

The pig grunted again.

Godfrey sighed. What a stupid creature, he thought. I'll give it one more go.

"The farmer chopped his head off. With an axe," he said, slowly and clearly. "I suppose you wouldn't know why?"

The pig gave a huge yawn. Then it said in a bored voice, "Born yesterday, were you?"

"No," said Godfrey. "I'm nearly six weeks old."

"Ah well," said the pig, "you've still got a bit of time left then."

"Time left?" said Godfrey. "Before what?"

"Before your head's chopped off too. It will be, once you're big enough."

"Big enough for what?"

"Big enough to eat," said the pig. "Humans eat chickens, didn't you know? Your dad finished up on a plate. Like we all shall, one day."

"Oh," said Godfrey. "Do people eat pigs too?"

"Sure. And they eat cows. And sheep. Haven't you ever heard the well-known expression 'as greedy as a human'? Or 'as fat as a human'? When I was a piglet and was gobbling my food, my father always used to say to me, 'Stop making a human of yourself'. He was an awful boar, my father."

"I never talked with my father," said Godfrey sadly, "and now I never shall."

The pig snorted, with amusement, it seemed.

"Not unless he comes back," it said.

"Comes back?" said Godfrey. "What do you mean?"

"His ghost, I mean," said the pig.

"What is a ghost?" said Godfrey.

"A spirit. The shape of the one who has died, returning to its earthly home. They come at night, and they're usually a ghastly pale colour."

Like Daddy, thought Godfrey. He was pure white.

"Have you ever seen one?" he asked.

"No," said the pig. "Personally, I'm not the type. Some can see ghosts, some can't. Most are terrified by them."

"But why does a ghost come back?" said Godfrey.

"Because it's sad. And angry. Angry at being sad. So it returns to haunt the place where it once lived."

"Oh," said Godfrey. "I see. Well, thanks for telling me."

"Don't mention it," said the pig. "And I'm sorry about your dad. Just remember one thing, any time you see the farmer with his axe in his hand . . ."

"What?" said Godfrey.

"Don't lose your head."

That night Godfrey sat on his perch in the henhouse, pondering. Why had his father died? Because humans liked to eat meat and the farmer and his family were humans, so they had eaten his father.

Why, thought Godfrey, must humans eat meat? Chickens didn't, after all – they managed all right without it, so why couldn't humans? If only they didn't eat chickens, then he and his brothers and sisters and his mum would have nothing to fear. If only these particular humans could be persuaded to change their ways. But how?

And at that precise moment, as Godfrey sat wide awake thinking, while all around him in the dark henhouse the rest of the chickens slept, he saw, coming through the pophole, a white shape.

The pophole was closed, of course, to keep the flock safe from the fox, but the shape came right through the wood of the little door, floated through, it seemed to Godfrey, and swam up to land on an empty perch opposite him.

It was the shape of a fine white cockerel – it was the shape of his father, looking exactly as he had in life except for one thing. The proud neck ended abruptly, in nothing. His father, Godfrey could see, was carrying his head tucked underneath his wing.

"Daddy!" said Godfrey softly, so as not to wake the others. "Speak to me!"

With the tip of its free wing the ghost touched first the top of its neck and then its head.

"You mean you can't speak?" said Godfrey, and he saw his father's beak rise and fall as the head nodded.

"But it is you? I mean, it is your ghost?"

The head nodded again.

36

At that minute a great idea occurred to Godfrey.
The pig had said that most of those who saw
ghosts were terrified by them. Suppose the farmer
was? Suppose he got such a shock that he never
again . . .!

"Daddy!" Godfrey said. "Can you make yourself
invisible?"

The ghost vanished.

"And then reappear?"

The ghost did.

"Listen then, Daddy," said Godfrey, and he
outlined his plan.

So it was that next morning when the farmer

came and opened the pophole door, all the flock hastened out of the henhouse, except one.

Hidden in the straw of a nesting box, Godfrey let out the most awful noise he could manage, the sort of noise, he hoped, that a ghost might make if it still had its head on. It was a kind of a scream and a screech and a squeak and a squeal all rolled into one.

"What the devil is that?" said the farmer, and he flung open the main door of the henhouse and looked in.

And as he looked, there suddenly appeared in the gloom of the interior a fine white cockerel, carrying its head tucked underneath its wing. For a moment the eyes in that head stared unblinkingly into the farmer's own.

Then, as Godfrey watched from his hiding place, his father's ghost floated slowly off its perch towards its murderer.

"You should have heard the man shout!" said Godfrey later to the pig. "You should have seen him run!"

"Wonder what he said to his wife," grunted the pig.

*

"Never again! Never again!" said the farmer to his wife in a voice that shook with horror.

"Never again what?" she asked.

"Chicken," said the farmer. "We're never going to eat chicken again, none of us, never, do you understand?"

"But why?"

"Never you mind."

There was a puzzled expression on the face of the farmer's wife.

"You look like you've seen a ghost," she said.

Glued to the Telly

Jamie Rix

Herbert Hinckley loves the television. He doesn't go to school. He doesn't go out to play. He doesn't have any friends. He doesn't need them, because Herbert Hinckley really loves the television.

He sits all day in his shabby red armchair, eating packets of crisps and drinking Coca Cola. His parents don't seem to mind. So long as Herbert is happy, they are happy. So Herbert just sits there, day in day out, flicking between the channels, watching programme after mindless programme on a battered old television set.

If you ask Herbert what any of the programmes are about, he always replies, "Cheese and Onion". When Herbert watches the television, all he can think about is the flavour of his next packet of crisps.

The television set is as old as Herbert himself. His parents bought it for him on the day that he was born. It has seen better days. The back is held on with rubber bands and garden string. The knobs on the front have long since dropped off and been replaced by lumps of half-chewed bubble gum. The screen has got a crack across it, that Herbert mended with Sellotape and sticking plaster.

"Would you like to sleep down here tonight, Herbert, as a treat?" said his mother one day.

"Cheese and Onion," said Herbert.

"We thought you'd like to," said Mr Hinckley. "You can watch the television all night if you sleep down here."

"It'll make a nice change for you," said his mother, taking away the empty crisp packets, and pushing a fresh bag into Herbert's lap.

Although you'd never have known it, Herbert was very excited as his parents made up the sofa in the sitting room.

"Sleep well, dear," said Mrs Hinckley.

"Salt and Vinegar," said Herbert, who was obviously enjoying himself, because the last time he had asked for Salt and Vinegar, England were winning a test match against the West Indies.

Herbert sat in his armchair until the little white dot disappeared from the screen. Then he got up and switched the television off at the mains. It was an old set, so this was a wise precaution. He didn't want any fires starting while he was asleep. He looked at the newspaper to check what time the Breakfast Show started, set his alarm, and climbed into bed, exhausted after a hard day's watching.

He dreamed of cheese and onion crisps.

An hour later, while Herbert slept, a silver grey cloud passed between the moon and Herbert's house. The sitting room was plunged into total darkness. A streak of lightning cracked through the sky and struck the aerial that led directly into the back of Herbert's television. A switch clicked on. A faint humming sound grew from deep inside the belly of the machine. Then suddenly, BLIP! The television switched itself on. The little white dot that had been no bigger than a fingernail started to grow, getting larger and larger with every sleepy breath that Herbert took. It was as if Herbert and the television were breathing as one. The dot filled the screen and spread out into the room. It crept across the floor towards the sofa, edged over Herbert's pillow and on to his face. Herbert half opened one eye, but it was too late.

The blinding light had completely surrounded him and suddenly, like a fisherman's net, it snatched him up and dragged him back through the television screen.

"Good morning, Herbert," said Mrs Hinckley when she came downstairs the next morning. "Crisps for breakfast?" She stopped at the door to the sitting room. "Herbert?" She went in and looked behind the curtains. "Herbert?" Mr and Mrs Hinckley could not find Herbert anywhere.

"He's probably turned into a television set!" laughed Mr Hinckley.

"That's not funny, George," said his wife, but she peered into the television screen just in case.

Herbert got the shock of his life when he opened his eyes and saw his mother's face pressed up against the outside of the screen. She looked like a giant goldfish, only goldfish didn't have bad teeth and a big nose.

"Cheese and Onion!" he said to her, but she couldn't hear him. In fact she couldn't see him either, because he was only six inches tall. He was all alone inside his own television set.

It was very dark, except for a flashing red light at the end of a narrow passage. His way forward was blocked by a big metal coil that hummed like

a top. When Herbert tried to pick it up, it burned his hand. He lay down on the floor, braced himself against an electrical circuit board and kicked the coil as hard as he could. It snapped off and shot a jagged blue spark into the ceiling, where it fizzed and crackled. Then he rolled over and crawled up the passageway towards the flashing light.

As he got closer he saw a door. He could hear a voice as well, which was strangely familiar. It was as if he'd heard it once in a dream. He eased down the door handle and slipped into the room.

Inside there was a lady, sitting behind a desk. She was shuffling and re-shuffling thousands of bits of paper. She turned towards Herbert as he came in, and he instantly recognized her. It was Gayna Honeycombe, his all-time favourite news-reader! But what was she doing talking to herself?

"The mystery of disappearing television addict, Herbert Hinckley, continues today."

Herbert's ears nearly dropped off the side of his head. Gorgeous Gayna was talking about him!

"His parents have expressed concern for his health. They are worried that he won't be able to find enough packets of Cheese and Onion crisps to keep his strength up. Apparently, Herbert likes to eat at least fifty packets a day. And now the main points of the News again . . ."

Herbert was in love and he didn't care who knew it. The gentle waft of Gayna's perfume had sent his love buds into frantic activity. His mouth was drooling. His arms were outstretched. He ran to-wards his screen goddess calling out her name for all the world to hear.

And she ignored him.

She never once looked up. In fact she went one further than that. As Herbert threw himself across the desk into her arms, she vanished. She completely disappeared, along with the desk and her bits of paper.

"How very odd," thought Herbert. It was just as if somebody had switched Gayna off. Well, somebody had – Herbert's mother. She wanted to watch the Cowboy film on the other side.

Suddenly, an electric cable snapped off the panel above Herbert's head, and crashed down into a bank of green bulbs, sending a shower of glass all over him. The cable thrashed wildly like a dying fish, then it was still.

Herbert gulped. The old television set was collapsing under his extra weight. He ran into a rusty corridor. Puddles of deadly acid oozed up from beneath the metal floor, and lumps of solder dangled precariously from the ceiling like so many dead spiders. The inside of Herbert's television was a mess. He had to get out of there.

There were hundreds of doors in the corridor. Herbert opened one. A little girl and a clown were sitting in the corner, listening to horrible, soupy music on an old gramophone.

"Get out," said the little girl. "Can't you see we're playing noughts and crosses?"

"Cheese and Onion," said Herbert. What he meant to say was sorry. He backed out and tried the next room along.

As he opened the door, a bullet whistled past his

nose and buried itself into the wall behind his left ear. A heavy fist thumped him on the end of his chin, and a large pair of hands picked him up and flung him halfway across the room.

"Howdy there, stranger," said the bartender. "Enjoying the fight?"

Herbert was still slightly dazed as he looked up. He was in a Wild West saloon bar, in the middle of the roughest, toughest brawl he had ever seen. The bartender ducked as a bottle smashed into the mirror behind him.

"What you having, pardner?" he said to Herbert. "Whisky?"

"A packet of Cheese and Onion crisps, please," replied Herbert. He was famished.

A very large, hairy man suddenly appeared next to him. "I'm going to hit you with my sledge-hammer," he said. "Would you like that?"

Herbert dived behind the bar as the large hairy man turned a perfectly nice bar stool into match-wood.

"It gets worse every night," said the little orange bear, who was also taking cover behind the bar. His doggy friend squeaked in agreement. "I mean why do they have to hurt each other? By the way I'm Sooty," said the bear, "and this is my friend Sweep."

"Pleased to meet you," said Herbert. "I'm Herbert Hinckley. I'm a great fan of yours. I've seen all your films. What are you doing behind this bar?"

"We're waiting to do our show," said Sooty wearily. "We can't start until they've finished fighting. Our viewers will be furious, you know. They want water pistols, not guns. They want to see custard pies pushed in people's faces, not chairs broken over some poor fellow's back. I mean look . . ." Sooty picked up a tiny chair and smashed it over Herbert's head. ". . . that's just not funny, is it?" said Sooty.

"No," said Herbert, "not really." Then his eyes rolled upwards and he crashed to the floor. Sooty had knocked him out.

When he came to, Herbert's arms appeared to be trapped by his side, but upon opening his eyes, he discovered that he was tucked up in a hospital bed. A doctor and a nurse were standing over him and gazing at each other.

"Nurse Pagett," said the doctor.

"Yes, Dr Miles," replied the nurse with a tear in her eye.

"The whole world thinks we're mad," said the doctor, "but we're not. I can't help myself, but I love you, Nurse Pagett."

"And I love you, Dr Miles!" she sobbed.

"Please, call me Tim," said the doctor.

Herbert didn't know where to look as Doctor Miles and Nurse Pagett threw their arms around each other and started kissing. It was like a scene out of one of those terrible television soap operas.

In fact it was one of those terrible television soap operas. That was why everyone had an Australian accent.

The door burst open and a woman rushed in. She was also crying. "I'm the boy's mother!" she wept.

She didn't look anything like Herbert's mother. "Is my son going to live?"

The doctor put the nurse down and put his arms round this strange woman instead.

"Sit down," he said (now there were tears in his eyes). "I'm afraid your son will never recover."

"Never recover!" shouted Herbert sitting up in bed. "I feel fine! I wouldn't mind a packet of Cheese and Onion crisps, but otherwise I've never felt better."

"But that's the problem!" said the doctor, turning to Herbert for the first time. "It is an absolute medical certainty that by six o'clock tomorrow morning, you will be a fully fried up Cheese and Onion crisp!"

"What!" shouted Herbert.

"Look at your fingernails," said the doctor. "They've already gone brown and crispy. Try one."

Herbert nibbled his thumb nail and screamed. It tasted just like a Cheese and Onion crisp. Delicious. He took a second bite, then suddenly leaped from his bed.

"What am I doing?" he shouted. "I'm eating myself!"

He was going to turn into his favourite food by the morning. How could he stop himself from eating himself all up? More to the point, how could he stop himself from turning into a crisp.

"Where are you going?" shouted the doctor, as Herbert crunched his way over to the door. He had one plan. Find a shower and stand underneath it all night. One thing that crisps weren't, was soggy. If he could keep himself soaking wet all night he couldn't possibly be a crisp, and if he wasn't a crisp there was no danger of him dying from being eaten by himself.

Herbert rushed from his hospital room and found himself back in the rusty corridor. As he ran in search of water, he tripped and fell against a metal grille. A tangle of red and green cables spilled out into a quivering heap on the floor. Sparks exploded from the cables and lit a circle of small fires.

Mr and Mrs Hinckley were still in the sitting room watching the television.

"I've seen enough of this hospital rubbish now," said Mrs Hinckley. "Let's turn over and watch the cookery programme on the other side. The one with that fat chef."

"Yes. I like him," said Mr Hinckley. "He's very funny." Then, "It's a shame Herbert's not here to see it."

They switched channels and didn't notice the

thin plume of smoke that had started to rise from the back of the television.

Herbert was still looking for a shower room, but it was getting more and more difficult to see where he was going as smoke billowed into the corridor. Shadowy figures rushed past in the opposite direction, shouting, "Fire! Fire! Get out before it's too late! Women, children and puppets first!"

"Stop!" shouted Herbert. "I need to find water before I turn into a Cheese and Onion crisp."

But nobody was listening. Even Batman and Robin ran past and pretended not to hear.

Mr and Mrs Hinckley had turned over to the cookery programme. The fat cook was showing everyone how to make potato crisps.

"Mmmm," said Mrs Hinckley. "Those look so good I can almost smell them."

The smoke was now rising steadily from the back of Herbert's television, and filling the room.

Herbert was banging on the back of the television screen. "Help!" he shouted.

He could see his parents sitting on the sofa, sniffing the air.

"Did you hear anything just then?" said Mr Hinckley.

"It was the cat," said his wife.

"I'm in the telly!" cried Herbert.

"Could you please get out of my way?" said the fat cook, who was standing behind Herbert in the kitchen. "People can't see what I'm doing."

"Tell them!" pleaded Herbert. "Tell them I'm in the television, there's smoke coming out the back, and I'm going to be turned into a Cheese and Onion crisp! They can't hear me."

The cook was not only fat, he was also mad. "You have smoke coming out of your back and you're a Cheese and Onion crisp?"

"No. I'm going to become a Cheese and Onion crisp!"

"If that's what you want," said the chef, picking Herbert up by the seat of his trousers, "why wait? Be a Cheese and Onion crisp now!" He opened the oven door and slid Herbert in.

Mr and Mrs Hinckley were laughing so much that they did not see the first flame leap out of the television set.

"That chef is so funny!" gasped Mr Hinckley. "Did you notice when he put that extra large potato into the oven?"

"It looked just like Herbert!" screamed Mrs Hinckley as she held her sides and went red in the face. "Oh look," she went on, pointing to the fire, which was now blazing out of the back of the television, "that chef is burning the crisps!"

Mr and Mrs Hinckley clutched each other, fell off the sofa and rolled around the carpet in a state of helpless hysteria. They were laughing so much that they never heard Herbert's cries for help.

When they stopped laughing, the television had gone. It had burned away to a pile of ashes. Sitting on the top was a big, fat Cheese and Onion crisp.

"Look at this mess," said Mrs Hinckley. "Whatever will Herbert say when he sees what's happened to his television set?"

"I'll buy him another one," said Mr Hinckley. "This one was getting a bit old anyway."

"I wonder where Herbert is?" said his mother, unwinding the flex to the vacuum cleaner.

"Probably gone out," said his father.

Mrs Hinckley started hoovering up the pile of ashes. "Well, he can't have gone far," she said. "He's left a crisp behind." She nibbled a corner. "Cheese and Onion. His favourite. I've never known him leave a Cheese and Onion. He's bound to come back to finish it."

She picked the crisp up, sealed it in a tupperware box, put it in the fridge and, unfortunately, forgot all about it.

The Monkeys

Ruskin Bond

I couldn't be sure, next morning, if I had been dreaming or if I had really heard dogs barking in the night and had seen them scampering about on the hillside below the cottage. There had been a Golden Cocker, a Retriever, a Peke, a Dachshund, a black Labrador, and one or two nondescripts. They had woken me with their barking shortly after midnight, and made so much noise that I got out of bed and looked out of the open window. I saw them quite plainly in the moonlight, five or six dogs rushing excitedly through the bracken and long monsoon grass.

It was only because there had been so many breeds among the dogs that I felt a little confused. I had been in the cottage only a week, and I was already on nodding or speaking terms with most of my neighbours.

Colonel Fanshawe, retired from the Indian Army, was my immediate neighbour. He did keep a Cocker, but it was black. The elderly Anglo-Indian spinsters who lived beyond the deodars kept only cats. (Though why cats should be the prerogative of spinsters, I have never been able to understand.) The milkman kept a couple of mongrels. And the Punjabi industrialist who had bought a former prince's palace – without ever occupying it – left the property in charge of a watchman who kept a huge Tibetan mastiff.

None of these dogs looked like the ones I had seen in the night.

"Does anyone here keep a Retriever?" I asked Colonel Fanshawe, when I met him taking his evening walk.

"No one that I know of," he said, and he gave me a swift, penetrating look from under his bushy eyebrows. "Why, have you seen one around?"

"No, I just wondered. There are a lot of dogs in the area, aren't there?"

"Oh, yes. Nearly everyone keeps a dog here. Of course every now and then a panther carries one off. Lost a lovely little terrier myself, only last winter."

Colonel Fanshawe, tall and red-faced, seemed to

be waiting for me to tell him something more – or was he just taking time to recover his breath after a stiff uphill climb?

That night I heard the dogs again. I went to the window and looked out. The moon was at the full, silvering the leaves of the oak trees.

The dogs were looking up into the trees, and barking. But I could see nothing in the trees, not even an owl.

I gave a shout, and the dogs disappeared into the forest.

Colonel Fanshawe looked at me expectantly when I met him the following day. He knew something about those dogs, of that I was certain; but he was waiting to hear what I had to say. I decided to oblige him.

"I saw at least six dogs in the middle of the night," I said. "A Cocker, a Retriever, a Peke, a Dachshund, and two mongrels. Now, Colonel, I'm sure you must know whose they are."

The Colonel was delighted. I could tell by the way his eyes glinted that he was going to enjoy himself at my expense.

"You've been seeing Miss Fairchild's dogs," he said with smug satisfaction.

"Oh, and where does she live?"

"She doesn't, my boy. Died fifteen years ago."

"Then what are her dogs doing here?"

"Looking for monkeys," said the Colonel. And he stood back to watch my reaction.

"I'm afraid I don't understand," I said.

"Let me put it this way," said the Colonel. "Do you believe in ghosts?"

"I've never seen any," I said.

"But you have, my boy, you have. Miss Fairchild's dogs died years ago – a Cocker, a Retriever, a Dachshund, a Peke, and two mongrels. They were buried on a little knoll under the oaks. Nothing odd about their deaths, mind you. They were all quite old, and didn't survive their mistress very long. Neighbours looked after them until they died."

"And Miss Fairchild lived in the cottage where I stay? Was she young?"

"She was in her mid-forties, an athletic sort of woman, fond of the outdoors. Didn't care much for men. I thought you knew about her."

"No, I haven't been here very long, you know. But what was it you said about monkeys? Why were the dogs looking for monkeys?"

"Ah, that's the interesting part of the story. Have you seen the *langur* monkeys that sometimes come to eat oak leaves?"

"No."

"You will, sooner or later. There has always been a band of them roaming these forests. They're quite harmless really, except that they'll ruin a garden if given half a chance . . . Well, Miss Fairchild fairly loathed those monkeys. She was very keen on her dahlias – grew some prize specimens – but the monkeys would come at night, dig up the plants, and eat the dahlia bulbs. Apparently they found the bulbs much to their liking. Miss Fairchild would be furious. People who are passionately fond of gardening often go off balance when their best plants are ruined –

that's only human, I suppose. Miss Fairchild set her dogs at the monkeys, whenever she could, even if it was in the middle of the night. But the monkeys simply took to the trees and left the dogs barking."

"Then one day – or rather, one night – Miss Fairchild took desperate measures. She borrowed a shotgun, and sat up near a window. And when the monkeys arrived, she shot one of them dead."

The Colonel paused and looked out over the oak trees which were shimmering in the warm afternoon sun.

"She shouldn't have done that," he said. "Never shoot a monkey. It's not only that they're sacred to Hindus – but they are rather human, you know. Well, I must be getting on. Good day!" And the Colonel, having ended his story rather abruptly, set off at a brisk pace through the deodars.

I didn't hear the dogs that night. But next day I saw the monkeys – the real ones, not ghosts. There were about twenty of them, young and old, sitting in the trees munching oak leaves. They didn't pay much attention to me, and I watched them for some time.

They were handsome creatures, their fur a silver-grey, their tails long and sinuous. They leaped gracefully from tree to tree, and were very polite and dignified in their behaviour towards each other – unlike the bold, rather crude red monkeys of the plains. Some of the younger ones scampered about on the hillside, playing and wrestling with each other like schoolboys.

There were no dogs to molest them – and no dahlias to tempt them into the garden.

But that night, I heard the dogs again. They were barking more furiously than ever.

"Well, I'm not getting up for them this time," I mumbled, and pulled the blankets over my ears.

But the barking grew louder, and was joined by other sounds, a squealing and a scuffling.

Then suddenly the piercing shriek of a woman rang through the forest. It was an unearthly sound, and it made my hair stand up.

I leaped out of bed and dashed to the window.

A woman was lying on the ground, and three or four huge monkeys were on top of her, biting her arms and pulling at her throat. The dogs were yelping and trying to drag the monkeys off, but they were being harried from behind by others. The woman gave another bloodcurdling shriek, and I dashed back into the room, grabbed hold of a small axe, and ran into the garden.

But everyone – dogs, monkeys and shrieking woman – had disappeared, and I stood alone on the hillside in my pyjamas, clutching an axe and feeling very foolish.

The Colonel greeted me effusively the following day.

"Still seeing those dogs?" he asked in a bantering tone.

"I've seen the monkeys too," I said.

"Oh, yes, they've come around again. But they're real enough, and quite harmless."

"I know – but I saw them last night with the dogs."

"Oh, did you really? That's strange, very strange."

The Colonel tried to avoid my eye, but I hadn't quite finished with him.

"Colonel," I said. "You never did get around to telling me how Miss Fairchild died."

"Oh, didn't I? Must have slipped my memory. I'm getting old, don't remember people as well as I used to. But of course I remember about Miss Fairchild, poor lady. The monkeys killed her. Didn't you know? They simply tore the poor woman to pieces . . ."

His voice trailed off, and he looked thoughtfully

at a caterpillar that was making its way up his walking stick.

"She shouldn't have shot one of them," he said. "Never shoot a monkey – they're rather human, you know . . ."

Beezlebub's Baby

Joan Aiken

Aunt Ada came to live with us at the end of the
summer holidays. Before, we'd only seen her
at Christmas and didn't realize just how awful she
was. Now, we had her all the time.

She was tall and pale with a face like a melon
and hair done in a grey knob on top of her head.
Her eyes were the colour of cherrystones. Her
skirts came almost to her ankles. And her voice
went non-stop.

"Don't you eat that orange in here, miss! Take it
in the garden. Let me see those hands, young man.
Just as I thought. You go straight off and wash
them. *What* is that *dog* doing on that *bed*?"

"Can't you stop her, Mum?" I asked, but Mum
said helplessly, "She is your father's elder sister,
you see . . ."

Dad, who is a merchant seaman, went to sea for

longer and longer trips.

Aunt Ada had Stuart's room, and Stu had to move in with Kev. I was lucky being a girl, I had a room of my own. At least I thought I was lucky . . .

Aunt Ada took over the shopping from Mum, she said that was only fair. What wasn't fair, she expected me to help her, after I got home from school.

Which was why we were coming out of the Dick Turpin shopping mall at half-past five on a cold October afternoon, each carrying two frightfully heavy bags of shopping.

"No use waiting for a bus, love," said a man at the Swilly Valley Service stop. "They're out on strike."

"Disgraceful!" said Aunt Ada, and she carried on and on about the wicked ways of bus drivers.

"We'd better start walking," I said sadly. "It's only a mile and a half."

"We'd best go along the tow-path," said Aunt Ada. "That's only half the distance."

"Oh no, don't let's do that," I said in a great hurry.

"Why ever not?" snapped Aunt Ada, staring at me with her cherrystone eyes.

"Because – because it's sure to be muddy."

"Don't be ridiculous, child! It hasn't rained all week. Come along and don't argue. I never *met* such children for argument."

"*Please* don't let's go that way," I said again. Dusk was beginning to thicken along Potter's Road; by the time we got to the canal bridge, it would be quite dark.

"Quiet, miss! I don't want to hear another word. Come along now – step out! Don't show me that sulky face."

And she stomped on ahead, every now and then turning round to glare at me, and make sure that I was following.

Well, I thought, she'll see it first. That's one comfort.

Another comfort was that our dog Turk wasn't with us. Turk will never, ever go along that stretch of the tow-path; he just turns round and runs home if anyone tries to take him that way, even in broad daylight.

By the time we got to the canal bridge, it was fully dark. And I could hear the sound long before we got there.

So could Aunt Ada.

"That's funny," she says. "I can hear a baby crying. Can *you* hear a baby, Janet?"

66

"Yes," I said glumly, because I could.

"This is *no* time of day for a baby to be out," said Aunt Ada. "Its mother ought to be ashamed of herself! I've a good mind to tell her so."

I didn't think its mother would have bothered much about Aunt Ada's bad opinion even if she had heard it, two hundred years ago.

"Where can that baby be? Can it be under the bridge?" Aunt Ada said.

As we drew near, the street-lights up above shone down on the path, and made the blackness under the bridge seem even blacker. And the crying became louder and angrier.

"*I* believe," said Aunt Ada, "*I* believe that some-body's *left* that baby under the bridge. Well – that somebody is going to be in bad, bad trouble!"

And she stepped into the darkness under the bridge. I lagged back, but she called, "Come *on*, Janet!"

Still, I was far enough back so that I could see the baby, all wet and dripping, and with a faint shine about it, like a dead fish that's gone bad, come climbing out of the canal water and run to Aunt Ada.

She dropped both her shopping bags; oranges and yoghurt cartons and toilet rolls shot in all directions.

I had expected that Aunt Ada would run off, screaming blue murder. Most people do that, when they see a ghost baby. But not she.

"Why, you poor, poor little mite!" she said. "Who *put* you in that water? Who did such a dreadful thing?"

"It was his mother—" I began to say. "She was a highwayperson two hundred years ago – she was called Beezlebub Bess—"

But Aunt Ada was taking no notice of me. She was cosseting that baby, patting it and cluck-ing over it like a hen that finds a diamond egg in the nesting box.

"*You'll* have to manage the shopping the rest of the way, Janet," she says to me. "I have to carry this poor little half-drowned angel."

And she picks up the ghost baby. Angel it certainly was not.

I don't think anyone had ever picked it up before. Mostly they run for their lives. A few have dropped dead on the spot. The baby wasn't at all used to being picked up. It struggled.

"None of that, now!" she said, gripping it firmly. And to me, "Poor thing, it's as light as a feather. Half starved, I daresay. Come *on*, Janet, look sharp, pick up those bags and let's be off. The sooner this little angel is into some dry clothes the better."

"But you can't take it to our home!" I said.

"Why ever not?" She was striding away along the path as fast as her long skirts would allow. She didn't stop to listen to me.

"It's a highwaylady's baby! She dropped it in the canal when the Bow Street runners were chasing her. Her name was Beezlebub Bess!"

Aunt Ada paid no heed; so I didn't go on to tell her that Bess's black horse Jericho had jumped clean over the twenty-foot canal and so helped its mistress escape from the runners. What became of her after that was never known. But the baby which fell into the canal was drowned, and had been making a ghostly nuisance of itself ever since on the tow-path. Some people call it the Wicked Baby, and not for nothing.

"You can't take it home!" I repeated.

But Aunt Ada did.

"I *really* don't think we can have that baby in our house," said Mum helplessly.

Mum is helpless just when she ought to be firm.

"And what Edward will say I can't imagine," she added.

"Edward won't be home for five months," Aunt Ada said. "And the baby can sleep in Janet's room."

My room! But Aunt Ada went to the United Baptists' Jumble Sale and bought a carrycot for 50 pence.

At night the baby was a real menace. When it wasn't crying, grizzling, or whimpering, it would be out of the cot and fidgeting around the room. Nothing was safe. Books and tapes fell off shelves, bottles and pots rolled off the chest-of-drawers, clothes were dragged off hangers, and in the middle of the night I'd feel its tiny little ice-cold fingers scrabbling at me or pulling my hair.

How would you like to share your bedroom with a ghost baby?

Turk wouldn't come in my bedroom any more, not even into the house, he stood and growled in the back doorway.

Elsewhere in the house, the baby was just as much of a hazard. One look from it was enough to send the TV into spirals. The lights fused if it crawled across the room; and a chicken that Mum put in to roast came out frozen instead, just because little Beezlebub went and peered in the oven ten minutes before dinnertime.

The boys and I couldn't stand it any longer. We wrote to Dad. He phoned from Cairo and told Aunt Ada that she must find somewhere else to live.

To our amazement this didn't faze her at all.

"I've already thought of that," she told him calmly. "I have applied for sheltered Council accommodation for me and my little angel. And I am pleased to say that they have put me at the top of the waiting-list."

Another month went by; but we felt we could bear it now, so long as we knew that it wouldn't be for ever. We could bear the baby's tearing up the mail in the letterbox, and eating Turk's dinner out of his bowl, turning the washing in the machine bright scarlet, making Mum's cake-mix taste as salty as the Sahara. We could bear the neighbours grumbling because it howled all night long, and the gasman refusing to call because he got his ankles bitten, and sending huge estimated bills.

We could bear the freezing cold in the house, and fish swimming in the bath.

We could bear it all if we knew the pair were going.

Well, in the end, Aunt Ada did go to her sheltered accommodation. But, guess what? The baby wouldn't stay there. She took it there OK, but it comes right back. It drifts through windows, it slides through keyholes. Night after night, there it is in my room, grizzling, scrabbling, rummaging in my drawers, poking me with its icy little fingers. The neighbours still complain, but what can we do?

It's got fond of us, see.

The Tourists

Jon Blake

It was like this, Miss Waiters. I'd just got home from school and I was just about to start on my homework. But my hand was still aching from all the work I'd done in lessons. So I chucked my bag down in the hall, went into the front room and switched on the telly.

That was when this feeling came over me. It was a feeling that I was not alone. It was a feeling that someone, or something, was watching me.

I looked around. There were twelve people round our standard lamp, carrying suitcases and cameras. The man at the front was wearing a blazer with a badge on it. He told me his name was Mr Runnymede from the Sun Fun Travel Agency. He asked if it was all right to take pictures.

"No, go ahead," I said, because I was that surprised, I couldn't think of anything else.

The strange people strolled round the room, flash-guns popping. They took it in turns to be photographed standing next to me. They were very friendly, but they spoke in slow, loud voices, as if I was deaf and stupid.

"IS-YOUR-HAIR-NATURALLY-WAVY?"

"DO-YOU-HAVE-A-SCHOOL?"

"IS-YOUR-FACE-NORMALLY-THIS-RED?"

Somebody noticed my bag in the hall. They all went out to look at it. They took endless pictures of it and asked if it was a local custom to throw bags on the floor. Some of them decided to throw their camera cases down in the same way. Then the whole crowd wandered off towards the broom cupboard, with Mr Runnymede pointing out this and that, and asking if the people at the back could hear.

I decided to stay calm. Then, after I'd stayed calm for a while, I decided to panic instead. I ran through the house, screaming for Mum and Dad.

I found Mum and Dad in the kitchen. Dad was lifting Grandad's old tin bath on to the cooker. Mum was arranging chairs and stools and garden seats round the table. They looked well flustered.

Before I could say a word, Mum had pushed a

piece of paper into my hand. "Take this list to the Co-op, will you, love?" she said.

"Hang on," I said. "Who are all these people?"

"Tourists," said Dad.

"Why are they in our house?"

"Don't ask me," said Dad, "but there may be a few bob in it."

I looked at the piece of paper in my hand. It said 50 tins of baked beans, 15 loaves of sliced bread, 10 kilos of sugar, 10 kilos of butter, 30 packets of tea and 25 jumbo toilet rolls.

"I should take the wheelbarrow," said Mum.

By the time I got back with the groceries, the tourists had moved into the kitchen. A small group were poking about in the fridge, discussing the contents of the ice-box. Others were examining the tea-towels, or touring the pantry. Soon, however, all the attention was on me and the wheelbarrow. Cameras clicked madly. Everyone agreed it must be another local custom.

Dad emptied the 50 tins of beans into Grandad's old tin bath. Mum cooked the toast in the toaster, the grill and the electric fire. Soon the tourists were wolfing it down, all except Mrs Pendleberry. Mrs Pendleberry was a stony-faced woman in a loud flowery dress. She didn't like the table-mats and she didn't like the candle stumps stuck on saucers. Most of all she didn't like baked beans. She said she didn't care if it was the local custom to eat beans. She was allergic to vegetables and only ate the tenderest veal.

Mr Runnymede the travel agent did his best to calm Mrs Pendleberry. Every time she took a swig of wine, he filled her glass again. Soon she was so drunk she couldn't tell the difference between baked beans and the tenderest veal. In fact, she couldn't even tell the difference between baked beans and the pattern on the plate. She ate everything.

After dinner, the tourists stayed at the table and talked. They talked about the best holiday they'd ever had, then the worst holiday they'd ever had, then the most in-between holiday they'd ever had. They swapped photos of the Pyramids and the Parthenon and the Hotel Paradiso. They told old jokes and sang *Y Viva Espana* and *The Birdy Song*. Then they climbed over the mountain of washing-up and went to view the night sky.

"Can we have our dinner now?" I moaned.

"What dinner?" said Mum.

"They've eaten it," said Dad. "They've eaten everything."

"But I'm starving!"

Dad laid a hand on my shoulder. "Not to worry, son," he said. "They're only here for two days, then they're off to the Taj Mahal."

My new duties did not end with the washing-up. Just as I was drying the last plate, Mr Runnymede returned with three tourists.

"This is Mr Hampsten, Mr Pettigrew and Mr Dark," he said. "They wonder if someone might show them upstairs. I have offered to do it, but they would prefer a local guide. Mr Pettigrew once climbed the Himalayas and he swears by local guides."

Mum and Dad decided this was just the job for me. The three tourists handed me their suitcases, and I struggled up the stairs like an old pack mule. The tourists followed, arguing about the height of various mountains.

"Bathroom," I snapped, kicking open the bathroom door.

The three tourists were puzzled. Even though I was speaking perfect English, they couldn't make head or tail of it. They went to the doorway and took a look for themselves.

"Ah," said Mr Pettigrew. "The bathroom."

We shuffled round our tiny landing, looking in

each of the rooms in turn. The tourists agreed that they were all very cute and quaint. I left my room till last, hoping they might have lost interest by then, but no such luck.

"*My* bedroom," I snapped, as the door swung open.

This time the three tourists did not stand in the doorway and peer inside. They walked straight in. Mr Hampsten closed the curtains, Mr Pettigrew asked me to leave the cases by the wardrobe, and Mr Dark tested the springs on the bed.

"Yes," he said. "This will do fine."

"Yes," said the others. "Perfect."

So saying, the three tourists climbed into bed, two upwards and one downwards, and in no time all three were snoring peacefully.

I hadn't forgotten about my homework. My plan was to do it early in the morning, when everything was quiet. Unfortunately, next morning our house was more like Waterloo Station. People were barging this way and that with razors and towels, and Mrs Pendleberry was banging on the bathroom door like a battering-ram. The air stank of stale fags, poo and toothpaste. Mum and Dad stood stranded in the crowd, holding camp-beds and pillows. I tried to avoid them but I couldn't move either way.

"Stan," said Mum, "get yourself in that kitchen. There's packed lunches to be made."

"But, Mum!" I protested. "I've got to go to school!"

"That's a poor excuse if ever I heard one."

The reason everything was so hectic was that the tourists were going on a coach trip. It was my job to wrap their apples and sarnies, while they packed their day-bags with insect cream, travel-sick pills, binoculars and sun-tan oil. Mr Runnymede was almost run off his feet. First he assured Mrs Pendleberry that the driver was a very careful man, who wouldn't even overtake a bike. Then he assured Mr Pettigrew that the driver was a former Grand Prix champion, who regularly broke the sound barrier down the M4. Then he put on his driving-gloves and rushed off down the bus station to get the coach.

Nothing had ever rolled up our road like that coach. It was massive, silver and blue, with toilet, video, polaroid windows and recliner seats. On the side it said TRANS-EUROPE DELUXE. The curtains stirred next door, and Mr and Mrs Redfern peered out jealously.

The tourists filed out of the house, clutching their packed lunches. Mr Runnymede ticked off their names and showed them to their seats. At last, they were off. We heaved a sigh of relief. Then we pattered back to the kitchen to see if they'd left us any toast.

"They're not such a bad crowd, really," said Mum.

"Mr Dark gave me a tip," said Dad. He showed us a small foreign coin.

At this point, I got another of those strange feelings. It was a feeling that things were just a bit too good to be true. For no particular reason, I looked out of the kitchen window. The big silver and blue coach was just drawing up at our back gate.

Off got Mr Runnymede. Off got the tourists. There was a quick name-check. Then Mr Runnymede opened the gate and the tourists filed happily into our back garden.

"Isn't this cute?" said Mr Hampsten.

"Isn't this quaint?" said Mr Pettigrew.

"And how unusual," said Mr Dark, "to find a garden without a swimming-pool."

The tourists each selected a spot. Then they spread napkins on the ground, opened their packed lunches and polished them off straight away. Mrs Pendleberry complained that there was a maggot in her apple. She hadn't actually seen it, but she just knew it was waiting for her.

After the picnic the tourists all sat up keenly, as if they were expecting something. Nothing happened. The tourists carried on waiting, now and then checking their watches.

"I can't wait for the entertainment," said Mr Hampsten.

"I wonder if it will be a local folk dance," said Mr Pettigrew.

"Or an unusual local sport," said Mr Dark.

"I hope there will be no flaming tar barrels," said Mrs Pendleberry. "My best dress was ruined by a flaming tar barrel."

Still they waited. So did we. Mr Runnymede began to look impatient. He got up. Next second, he was at the back door.

"Hr-r-r-m," he coughed.

"Yes?" said Mum nervously.

"EN-TER-TAIN-MENT," said Mr Runnymede, in his loudest, slowest voice.

Mum looked at Dad. Dad looked at me. I looked at the cat.

"EN-TER-TAIN-MENT," said Mr Runnymede

81

again, doing a little dance and pretending to play a guitar.

"Ah," said Dad, "I know what you mean."

Mum and Dad had a whispered discussion, then disappeared. Mum came back with an extension lead and Dad came back with the telly. He carried it out to the back garden and plugged it in. The tourists whispered and shuffled. "Shh!" went Mr Runnymede.

We sat down in front of the telly and switched it on. It was football. Soon I was so carried away with the game that I had completely forgotten the tourists. Then Mrs Pendleberry coughed. I looked around. To my surprise, the tourists weren't watching the telly at all. They were watching us.

"Do we have to watch sport?" said Dad, after a while more.

"Not on my account," said Mum.

Dad got up. The tourists leaned closer. Dad switched over. There was a little round of applause. Dad scratched his head and sat down again.

The new programme was about the Lost Tribe of the Taraboom. It was the kind of thing Mum hated.

"Isn't 'Sons and Daughters' on?" she asked.

Mum jumped up and switched over again. The

telly went funny. Mum gave it a whack. Suddenly there was a massive round of applause.

"Bravo!" said Mr Pettigrew.

"Olé!" said Mr Dark.

"I saw exactly the same act in Monte Carlo," said Mrs Pendleberry.

Mum looked surprised. Then a smile came to her face. She did a little curtsy. The tourists applauded again.

Dad's face grew jealous. He jumped to his feet. In one giant stride he was at the telly. He stabbed the off-button like a matador.

"*That's* what I think of 'Sons and Daughters'!" he stormed.

The crowd went wild. Dad turned to the right and bowed, then turned to the left and bowed again. Meanwhile Mum was back on her feet, dusting her hands together.

"And just who bought the television?" she snapped, switching it on again.

More applause. The tourists moved closer.

"Do you think there will be any blood?" asked Mrs Pendleberry.

"I certainly hope so," said Mr Hampsten.

Luckily there wasn't any blood, but Mum and Dad did shout themselves hoarse trying to out-act

each other. The telly went off, on, off, on, till I was sure it was going to explode. Then, out of the blue, Mr Runnymede checked his watch and jumped to his feet.

"Coach leaves in two minutes precisely!" he called.

The tourists quickly packed their bags and filed back through the gate, leaving a pile of silver foil and apple cores. Half a minute later they arrived at the front door, refreshed by their outing and ready for tea.

*

You've seen those films where a cloud of locusts arrives and they strip a field bare. Well, that was what our house was like after two days of the tourists. All traces of food had disappeared. Ashtrays and other small objects were also starting to disappear. The curtains and pictures had faded due to the endless camera flashes. A trail had been worn through the carpet towards the bathroom.

Now, at last, it was time for the tourists' farewell meal. Mum and Dad sent me down to the butchers for a sackful of steak and kidney. Unfortunately, by now the butcher had completely run out of meat. All he had was two dozen pork hocks, which he was going to give to his dogs. They were disgusting. They looked like something human. I bought them.

Mr Runnymede was making a speech when I got home. As usual, he was using lots of arm-waving and hand movements to make sure Mum and Dad understood.

"On behalf of the Sun Fun Travel Agency," he said, "may I say how very much we have enjoyed our stay at 364 Holway Green Road."

"It's so refreshing to find a place that hasn't been spoiled by tourists," added Mr Dark.

"In fact," said Mr Runnymede, "we have had such a good time, we have decided to stay another fortnight."

Mum and Dad said nothing, just stood there with their mouths open. The tourists swarmed round them, thanking them, and saying how much they were looking forward to the next two weeks.

I backed slowly out of the door. I quietly selected a hammer and nails from Mum's toolbox, then crept upstairs to nail myself into my room.

The light was on. There were noises inside. Gently I pushed open the door, to find myself face to face with Mrs Pendleberry. The contents of my tin chest were scattered over the floor, and in Mrs Pendleberry's hands was the old football-card album which my grandad gave me.

Mrs Pendleberry was not one bit embarrassed. She smiled in a put-you-down way and shook the album in my face.

"HOW-MUCH-YOU-WANT?" she asked.

"It's not for sale," I told her.

Mrs Pendleberry took out her purse and started showing me money. "I-GIVE-YOU-MONEY," she said. "I-GIVE-YOU-PLENTY-MONEY."

"I don't want money," I told her, but she carried on flashing the fivers all the same.

I suppose I could have just snatched the album from her and run away. But she'd only have come after me and kept bothering me. So I started thinking. A plan began to form in my mind. It was a plan which would rid us of Mrs Pendleberry, and all the other tourists, for good.

"Come with me," I said. "I've got ten more albums like that."

Needless to say, Mrs Pendleberry didn't understand. But after a few waving arms and hand movements, she got the message. She gathered up her bag and hobbled eagerly after me. We went down the stairs, along the hall and out into the back garden.

"Out here?" asked Mrs Pendleberry doubtfully.

"In there," I replied, pointing to the outside bog.

"In there?" asked Mrs Pendleberry, even more doubtfully.

Mrs Pendleberry prodded open the door and looked inside. She saw the rusty old cistern and the broken seat and the spiders' webs. She didn't much care for it.

"Behind the cistern," I explained, with the usual arm movements.

Mrs Pendleberry placed one nervous foot inside, then the other. In a flash I had slammed the door

and dropped the catch. All that could be seen of Mrs Pendleberry was a few inches of her dress, trapped in the door.

"Let me out of here!" she yelled. But her efforts were in vain. All she managed to do was rip the piece of dress. I picked it up and put it in my pocket. Then I strolled back in to help with the dinner.

It wasn't long before the other tourists noticed that Mrs Pendleberry had disappeared. They began wandering round the house, calling for her. They checked the bedrooms and the bathroom and even the airing cupboard. But no one checked outside, because Mrs Pendleberry hated the outdoors. It was always too hot, or too cold, or too in-between.

"What are we going to do?" said Mum. "We've cooked for twelve and there's only eleven."

"Just leave everything to me," I said.

With that, I picked up a plate, ladled out a pork hock and sat down at the table.

"Stan!" said Dad. "What do you think you're doing?"

At this point, the tourists arrived in the kitchen, still searching for Mrs Pendleberry. When they saw me, they stopped dead. They hadn't seen one of us eating before. Out came the cameras, and the binoculars, and Mr Runnymede's microphone.

"I wonder what he's eating," mused Mr Hampsten.

The tourists moved in closer, watching my fork all the way into my mouth and down again.

"It's very strange," says Mr Pettigrew.

I pick up the bone and chew it like a caveman.

"They eat dogs in Korea," says Mr Dark. "I do hope it's not a dog!"

I finish the last mouthful and let out a big burp. Then I reach into my pocket and pull out the torn piece of dress. "Good," I say, wiping it across my mouth.

"That's . . ." stammers Mr Hampsten.

". . . Mrs Pendleberry's dress!" exclaims Mr Pettigrew.

"What have you done with Mrs Pendleberry!" demands Mr Dark.

Suddenly a look of horror comes over the tourists. They stare at my face, then down to the empty plate, then back to my face again. I lick my lips.

"Cannibals!" yells Mr Hampsten.

"I knew we should have gone to Benidorm!" says Mr Pettigrew.

With that, the tourists flee the house, ignoring Mr Runnymede's frantic excuses. Mum and Dad stare after them, baffled, then shrug their shoulders and sit down to their first decent meal in three days.

"Is this *really* Mrs Pendleberry?" says Dad, mopping up the last of the gravy. "You know, she really doesn't taste too bad."

The New Nanny

Jamie Rix

There is a family, living in South London, that has the collective intelligence of a dead ant. Mr Frightfully-Busy spends all his time at the office and wears nasty pink ties to work. Mrs Frightfully-Busy helps out in a gift shop in the King's Road. She flits around the shelves all day doing absolutely nothing, trying to avoid serving any customers. Their children are called Tristram and Candy. They hardly know their parents, because their parents are never at home, and they spend most of their days being completely unpleasant to their long-suffering nanny.

Mrs Mac is sixty-three years old and was Mrs Frightfully-Busy's nanny when Mrs Frightfully-Busy was a child. Now Mrs Mac has to look after Tristram and Candy, which is no easy task.

In the morning when Mrs Mac dresses the

children, they lay traps for her by hanging their duvets over the door. Once she is entangled in their quilts, the children leap off the top bunk, tie her up with string and threaten to push her out of the window. When she cooks their lunch they put the bits they don't want on to her chair, so that when Mrs Mac sits down she gets fish fingers all over her bottom. At bath time they pretend to be asleep in the water. When she leans forward to wake them, they spit water in her face. When it is time for bed, they call her names, hide in the airing cupboard, switch on the telly, refuse to brush their teeth, pretend they are ill, find an interesting book that they want her to read, and run to their mummy and daddy to tell lies about how badly Mrs Mac looks after them. The worst thing is that their parents always believe their lies, because in their eyes Tristram and Candy can do no wrong.

One day Tristram and Candy went too far.

"Mrs Mac beat us today," they lied to their parents.

Mrs Frightfully-Busy looked up from her Martini. "She beat my precious little angels?"

"Yes," said Candy, "so hard that I cried."

"That's not on," said Mr Frightfully-Busy. "Remind me to tell Mrs Mac never to do it again."

"I should think so too," added Mrs Frightfully-Busy. "Now run along children, Mummy and Daddy want a little peace and quiet."

"She beat us with your golf clubs, Daddy."

"My golf clubs!" Mr Frightfully-Busy was out of his chair in a flash. "Did she break them?"

"Oh yes," whimpered Tristram, who was a very good actor, "across the back of my legs!"

"Those golf clubs cost me a fortune!" he shouted as he stormed out of the room. Then they heard him bellow from the foot of the stairs, "Mrs Mac. You're fired. Pack your bags and get out of this house at once!"

Poor old Mrs Mac. She had worked for the family for forty years and now she was being thrown out, because of one malicious, spiteful, childish lie.

The next day Mrs Frightfully-Busy was in a panic. There was nobody to look after her children and *she* certainly wasn't going to do it. She looked in the telephone directory under Nanny. All the agencies seemed to be exactly the same. All except one. *Animal Magic*, it read. *We provide nannies to suit* all *children. No child too difficult to handle.*

Mrs Frightfully-Busy phoned them up.

"They are the most adorable little children you

could ever wish to meet," she said to the voice at the other end of the phone. "Dear, sweet Tristram is so kind and gentle, and Candy is really no trouble at all. I hardly know she's there sometimes."

"There'll be somebody round in half an hour," said the voice and Mrs Frightfully-Busy heaved an enormous sigh of relief.

Half an hour later there was a ring at the door.

"Come and meet your new nanny," Mrs Frightfully-Busy shouted to Tristram and Candy, as she opened the front door. There was nobody there.

"Down here!" hissed a voice on the front path.

Mrs Frightfully-Busy looked down.

"Animal Magic Nannies at your service," added the thirty-five foot python as it slithered across the doormat and into the hall.

Tristram and Candy stopped dead at the foot of the stairs. Their jaws dropped open in disbelief. A long brown snake wearing a starched white apron, and carrying a suitcase, had just slid into their house. Their mother must have gone stark staring bonkers and, to cap it all, she hadn't even noticed.

"I'll be back at six! Have a good day," said Mrs Frightfully-Busy, picking her car keys up from the

hall table and sweeping out of the front door. The door slammed shut and Tristram and Candy were left alone with their new nanny.

"What would you like to do today, children?" said the python. Its red tongue darted in and out of its mouth. The children were too frightened to answer.

"Shall we play a game of snake and ladders?"

Candy couldn't help herself. She screamed. "Don't eat us."

"Eat you," said the snake. "Don't be silly. I'm here to look after you. Just treat me as you would any other nanny."

That was what Tristram and Candy needed to hear. From that moment on they reverted to their normal, horrible selves.

At lunch they stuck their nanny's tail in a pan of boiling water. In the park they scattered tin tacks on the path, which pierced her skin as she slithered over them. They wrapped her up in their parents' bath towels and stuck her head down the lavatory. They knotted her around the legs of their bunk beds and left her tied up all afternoon, while they watched the telly. They even staked her out in the back garden and waited for the birds to come down and peck at her, thinking she was an enormous worm.

By the time Mr and Mrs Frightfully-Busy came back that night, the new nanny was a nervous wreck. She was more scared of the children than they were of her. No sooner did she hear the front door open, than she was out of that house faster than a speeding bullet.

"How was the new nanny?" said Mr Frightfully-Busy.

"Really cruel," lied the children.

"Do you know," said Tristram, "she nearly strangled me when she gave me a hug."

"Then she's never coming back into this house!"

declared Mrs Frightfully-Busy.

The next morning Mrs Frightfully-Busy phoned Animal Magic again. "The nanny you sent yesterday was completely useless!" she said.

"Yes," said the voice at the other end, "I know. She's told us all about your children. We'll send you a more suitable nanny today. She'll drop in in about fifteen minutes."

Sure enough, fifteen minutes later the doorbell rang. Mrs Frightfully-Busy picked up her car keys and opened the door.

"Bye children. The new nanny's here. See you later." She didn't even stop to find out who the new nanny was.

Tristram and Candy rushed to the open door to see for themselves, but they could see no one.

"Cooee," said a voice above them. But before they could look up an enormous, hairy black spider dropped down from the roof of the porch.

"I'm the new nanny," said the spider as she bit through her web and scuttled into the hall. "You must be Tristram and Candy. I've heard so much about you."

Tristram and Candy had turned white.

"I h-h-h-hate spiders," stammered Tristram.

"Me too," agreed Candy.

"Don't be silly," said the spider. "I wouldn't harm a fly." She paused for a moment to think. "Well, maybe a fly, but I wouldn't harm you."

"Oh good," said Candy, who was already thinking up some awful prank to play on the spider.

"Now where shall we begin?" said the nanny.

"In the bathroom," fibbed Candy. "We always have a bath after breakfast."

So up to the bathroom they went.

It is a well-known fact that spiders hate water. The children's nanny was no exception. Her own father had nearly drowned once in a hand basin. Tristram and Candy deliberately kept splashing her.

"Stop it," she screamed.

The children gained the upper hand.

"Shan't!" shouted Tristram, filling a bucket full of water and pouring it over his nanny's head. She retreated into a corner and curled up into a furry ball. The children jumped out of the water, picked her up, threw her into the bath and pulled the plug out. The spider was caught in a raging whirlpool that sucked her down towards the drain.

Tristram and Candy poked her with a flannel and laughed.

The spider suddenly sprang open, her legs flailing about in the torrent, and with one mighty effort she clawed her way to the edge of the bath and climbed out. Tristram offered her his towel.

"What can we do now?" he smirked.

"I know," said Candy to the spider. "You can build us a climbing frame in the garden."

The new nanny was wet and miserable as she set about spinning the children a climbing frame. Every time she stopped to catch her breath, they shouted, "More! It's still not big enough!" until, finally, her web stretched from one garden fence to the other. At its highest point it reached the chimney pot on top of the roof, and it fell away steeply across the entire length of the garden to Mr Frightfully-Busy's compost heap. It looked like a circus safety-net – the sort trapeze artists use in the big top.

The spider collapsed at the end of her ordeal and fell asleep from exhaustion.

"A fine nanny she's turned out to be," said Tristram. "Let's teach her a lesson she'll never forget."

So they pulled down the climbing frame, and while she slept they wrapped her up in her own web.

That was how Mr and Mrs Frightfully-Busy found her. Cold and damp. The children's unlucky prisoner.

"This looks like a fun game," said Mr Frightfully-Busy. "What's it called?"

"Poke the nanny," said Candy prodding the spider with a sharp stick.

"What a super idea," said Mr Frightfully-Busy. Then, "Thank you, nanny, you can go now. We'll see you in the morning."

Mr Frightfully-Busy picked up the spider, put her in a wheelbarrow and dumped her on the pavement.

In bed that night, Tristram was asked what he thought of his new nanny. "Even crueller than the snake," he lied. "Do you know what she did? She tied her web around our ankles and hung us upside down from the ceiling all morning."

"We don't like her," chipped in Candy.

"Then she's never coming back into this house!" declared Mrs Frightfully-Busy.

The following morning she rang up the *Animal Magic Nanny Agency* for the third time. "I'll give you one last chance to send me a nanny who can look after my children properly!" she shouted down the phone.

"Yes, Mrs Frightfully-Busy. As it happens, we have the perfect nanny right here in the office. I'll send her over straight away," said the voice at the other end.

On this particular morning, Mrs Frightfully-Busy couldn't even wait for the new nanny to arrive. She just had to get off to work.

"I'll leave the door on the latch," she said to the children. "When the new nanny arrives, just tell her to come straight in." Then she pulled the door to and left Tristram and Candy alone in the house.

Seconds later they heard squelchy footsteps outside the front door.

"Come straight in!" shouted Tristram, who was standing on a chair waiting to bonk his new nanny on the head with a baseball bat as she came through the door.

The door swung open and the squelchy footsteps came in.

CLONK! Tristram brought the bat down hard on the nanny's head. Candy squealed with delight. It was such a clever trick.

Then they both stopped laughing. The new nanny blinked and continued walking. She stopped in the middle of the hall. Water dripped off her scaly back and formed tiny puddles on the carpet. She flicked her tail.

"I'm your new nanny," said the alligator. "Any nonsense, and I'll eat you for breakfast."

"We're not scared of you, are we?" said Candy, cockily.

"No way," said Tristram. "You're just the nanny. Take that!" and he hit the alligator on the head again.

It was all over in a flash. Two snaps, two gulps and the children were gone.

When Mr and Mrs Frightfully-Busy came home that night they couldn't find the children anywhere. Mrs Frightfully-Busy did, however, find a very sleepy alligator curled up in the airing cupboard. "Are you the nanny?" she said.

"Yes," said the alligator, opening one eye.

"Where are the children?" said Mr Frightfully-Busy, hiding behind his wife.

"I've eaten them," said the alligator, licking her lips. "Although I must say they tasted horrible, but then little liars always do."

"Get out of this house immediately!" shouted Mr Frightfully-Busy.

"That won't be necessary," replied the alligator, raising her head and flashing a fearsome set of teeth. She edged forwards and Mr and Mrs Frightfully-Busy backed away down the stairs. Then the alligator stood up on her back legs and just as they thought she was going to pounce, she laid two large, white eggs.

"Excuse me," said the alligator, brushing past Mr and Mrs Frightfully-Busy. "Places to go. People to see." And she left.

Mr Frightfully-Busy sat his wife down, then went over to the eggs to take a closer look. They each had a long crack down one side. As Mr Frightfully-Busy watched, the cracks grew bigger.

"The eggs are hatching!" he said to his wife. "We're about to be invaded by baby alligators!"

There was a crunch, then a snap. Something scraped against the edge of the shell. Then the first finger emerged, followed by an arm, a neck, then a head. It was Tristram.

"My baby!" shouted Mrs Frightfully-Busy rushing over and wrapping her arms round him.

Candy suddenly burst through the shell of the second egg.

"My two babies!" she wailed. "What happened?"

"We were rude and nasty to the nanny," said Tristram.

"And she ate us," added Candy.

It was the first time they had ever told the plain truth.

There was a ring at the front door. Mr Frightfully-Busy left his family to answer it. It was Mrs Mac.

"I was wondering if you'd found a new nanny yet for Tristram and Candy," she said.

"No," said Mr Frightfully-Busy.

"In that case, would you like me to come back?" said Mrs Mac.

Mr Frightfully-Busy didn't know what to say. Then he remembered the snake, the spider and that awful alligator. "Yes please," he said, without hesitation. "When can you start?"

"Right away," said Mrs Mac, "if you'll help me in with my things."

"Certainly," said Mr Frightfully-Busy, and he bent down to pick up her suitcases. One was made of snake skin. One was all black and hairy (and looked remarkably like a spider) and the third, the biggest of them all, was made from the skin of an alligator.

Cross-Purposes

Joyce Dunbar

Software Superslug wants to be a snail but first he needs a house. He thinks that the pouffe in the Potters' sitting room will be ideal. But each night when he goes to try it out, he leaves a shiny, slug trail behind him. Potty Mrs Potter thinks he's a super-intelligent snail. She's sure his super slug trail is actually a secret message, if only she could decode it . . .

"Bowed, but not defeated," said Software to himself when he returned to The Hole that morning. Those nightly expeditions to the sitting room had meant that he wasn't getting much to eat. He was looking rather thin for his size. "What I need to do now is build up my strength," he decided. So for several nights after that he went with the rest of the snails, dining out in the garden on bean sprouts and tulip shoots.

When almost a week had passed without a new pattern on the pouffe, Mrs Potter assumed that her visitor had left for good, which made her feel very down-hearted. But Mr Potter and the children were delighted. They'd had enough of snails. Besides, they had something else to think about.

It would soon be the school concert. Betsy was busy practising on her recorder, while Tom had some songs to learn. Mothers and fathers were invited of course, and Mrs Ponsonby-Froggat, as the Lady Mayoress elect and a former pupil of the school, was to be the guest of honour. She was also to give out prizes. All the children got a prize for something or other: thus, Betsy was getting a prize for her forward rolls in gymnastics, while Tom was getting the computer buff award.

Mrs Potter had a sense of occasion. She knew that this was an important event for her husband and the children and she wanted to show her support. She got out her best hat and two-piece, in matching cherry red.

The hat was in a turban style. "I don't think it's too old-fashioned," said Mrs Potter, trying on the hat at different angles. "I think it suits me rather well."

The evening before the concert Mrs Potter gave the two-piece and hat a good brush, then laid them on the sofa in the sitting room, all ready to put on.

Now it so happened that this was the very night when Software decided he was fit and strong enough to have another go at the pouffe. But my, oh my, when he saw the hat! It looked so much lighter than the pouffe, so much easier to get into! And the way it curled round and round! It looked tailor-made for a shell.

"It must be that nice Mrs Potter," he thought. "She must have left it for me as a present . . . and she's even laid out a red carpet!"

Grateful and touched to the heart, he crawled his way up the side of the sofa. He made a slow, stately, progress across the two-piece until at last he reached the hat.

Though a hat is much smaller than a pouffe, to a slug it looks very large. Software needed an overall view so that he could wear it at the most suitable angle. "There is an art in doing anything well," he thought, "even in the wearing of a shell."

So he crawled all the way round the outside of the hat until he reached the summit, where he paused to take a breath. Then he crawled all the

way back. It was a long, slow, process. Software
became very tired. By the time he reached the
inside he was so exhausted, and the hat was so very
snug, that he curled up and fell fast asleep.

When Mrs Potter came into the room in the
middle of the following morning, Software didn't
wake up.

When, at the sight of the shiny, slimy trail
running right across the two-piece and all around
the hat, Mrs Potter squealed, Software still didn't
wake up.

"Oh the pet!" she cried. "He's coming back! He's

left a message on my two-piece and hat! But oh dear! Now what shall I do?"

For Mrs Potter was faced with a problem.

Mr Potter and the children were already at the school and she was in a dreadful hurry. She tried to do a quick sketch of the slime, but there was just no time to get it right. She couldn't possibly wipe it off for she was sure it must be part of the code. And she hadn't anything else she could wear.

"There is nothing else for it," she said, smoothing down her hair, "I must wear my hat and two-piece as they are. It might even be a very good thing. Someone might see what it is. Someone might know what it means. With so many witnesses around, they won't think I'm dotty any more."

Taking care not to smudge the slime, she arranged the cherry turban on her head. Now she was really in a rush.

And so, though Software didn't know it, and Mrs Potter didn't know it, off to listen to a concert went a slug!

There was an empty seat at the front of the school hall. It was reserved for Mrs Potter. Her husband stood on the sidelines, doing the job of usher.

Between the empty seat and the headmaster, sat Mrs Ponsonby-Froggat, with an expectant smile on her face. The concert was about to begin.

It was then that Mrs Potter arrived, panting and out of breath. Nobody said a word, but oh, there were thoughts in heads!

"Cherry red," went one, "some people do like to get themselves noticed."

"Silver threads," went another, "and what a peculiar pattern."

"LATE!" went several others.

"She looks like a knickerbocker glory," one child actually whispered.

Mr Potter glanced at his wife, who had found her empty seat, and winced in absolute horror. She looked covered in runny nose!

Betsy and Tom, from their position on the stage, squirmed in embarrassment. Their greatest wish at that moment was for a mother like other children's mothers.

The conductor raised his hands. The recorders started to play. It was then that Software woke up.

"Where am I?" he wondered. "And what is that peculiar noise?"

"All things bright and beautiful," sang the children.

A second or so later some of the people sitting behind Mrs Potter noticed something very strange.

At first their eyes popped in surprise.

Then their mouths fell open.

Then they began to giggle.

The giggling was followed by nudging. The nudging led on to pointing. The pointing caused more staring. The result was more giggling than ever.

"All creatures great and small," sang the children on the stage, beginning to wonder what was so funny.

The giggling got worse and worse.

Mrs Potter wondered what the matter was and turned to Mrs Ponsonby-Froggat.

Mrs Ponsonby-Froggat wondered what the matter was and turned to Mrs Potter. She stared dumbstruck at the hat. She knew slime from silver threads, for she had seen it before on a pouffe.

What she saw next was worse.

A neat brown slug with outstretched tentacles peeped round from the side of the hat, took one look at Mrs Ponsonby-Froggat and hid itself in Mrs Potter's hair.

"All things wise and wonderful," the children soldiered on.

There was a ghastly scream and a very heavy thud. Poor Mrs Ponsonby-Froggat! She had fallen to the floor in a faint.

What a row in the car going home! Software listened to it all.

Mr Potter blathered and blustered at his wife for arriving late, for making a fool of him, for going completely bonkers.

The children grumbled and groused because the giggling had ruined their concert, sending them all out of tune. Then, when Mrs Ponsonby-Froggat had been carried off, the prize table had been upskittled and the headmaster had had to give out the prizes, which were all in a terrible muddle. Thus, Betsy had ended up with the sensible shoes award and Tom had got the tidiness prize.

Software wished he could join in. "What about me?" he wanted to say. "How do you think I felt? Waking up from a nap in a sea of human faces! It nearly frightened me out of my hat." But he thought he'd better save it for the snails.

Mrs Potter kept saying she was sorry, that she hadn't meant to spoil anything for anybody, that she'd no idea what had been so funny, and that if Mr Potter hadn't ushered her out so quickly they might have had a chance to find out. But the others went on and on until at last her hackles were up. Software felt the skin around her neck going tight and the hair roots standing on end. He shivered and tried not to sneeze. When Mrs Potter's hackles were up, it wasn't easy to put them down.

"IS there, or is there not, a snail in our sitting room?" she said between clenched teeth.

"Yes, but—"

"DOES it, or does it not, make patterns on our pouffe?"

"Yes, but—"

"ReMARKable, WONDerful, patterns?"

"Yes, but—"

"DOES this, or does it not, show a mind, intelligence, purpose?"

"Yes, but—"

"IS that, or is it not, EXTraordinary?"

"Yes, but—"

"PREcisely! And all that I do is take notice! You should take notice too!"

"Yes, but—"

"You've simply got a grudge against snails. This one is a GENIUS, I tell you. You've done too much school-teachering. Drawing straight lines with a ruler is all very well, but don't think your thoughts with one. They're sure to come out very dull. Something extraordinary is happening in our house and I am simply taking notice."

"But, Mum," protested Tom, "your hat looks covered in SNOT!"

"Don't SAY that disgusting word!" snapped Mrs Potter.

And for the rest of the journey home, the Potter family stayed silent. It was only as they got out of the car that Mrs Potter murmured, "Poor Mrs Ponsonby-Froggat. I wonder what made her pass out."

The Fine Art of
Wilderness Nutrition

Gary Paulsen

Gary Paulsen is an award-winning writer, best known for his extraordinary series of Hatchet *books. These books follow the fight for survival of Brian who, following a terrifying plane crash, finds himself alone in a hostile and dangerous environment. Gary Paulsen based Brian's adventures on his own experiences of surviving in terrible conditions. Here he tells about the fight to find food in the wilderness and how, when hungry, almost anything tastes good . . .*

Something that you would normally never consider eating, something completely repulsive and ugly and disgusting, something so gross it would make you vomit just looking at it, becomes absolutely delicious if you're starving.

Consider the British navy in the days of old sailing ships. Their principal food was hard tack, a dried biscuit kept in wooden barrels that were never quite airtight. After months and sometimes years at sea the biscuits would become full of maggots. The men spent many days trying to get rid of the worms, but once they were close to starving, they saw the maggots as food to smear on the biscuits, a kind of tasty butter. They would also eat the rats that hid in the ships' holds. By the end of a long voyage the rats could be sold to hungry sailors for up to a month's wages.

When I first started living on game, I thought only of grouse and rabbits and deer. I had thought I would eat only the best parts of the animal and stay away from anything disgusting. Like guts.

And I hung in with that thinking until I went about three days without making a kill, and when I finally did, it was a red squirrel, which is about the size and edibility of the common rat, though perhaps cuter. It was sitting on a tree limb about twenty feet away and I caught it with a blunt and dropped it and took it back to my camp and cleaned, skinned and gutted it. And then looked at it.

It looked as if I'd skinned a gerbil. I had a small aluminium pot and I put water in it and then the small carcass and boiled it for a time with some husked acorns I found. I ate it, along with the acorns, and I was cleaning the pot when I noticed the entrails on a log where I'd left them when I gutted the squirrel. My stomach was still empty, so I took the small heart and kidneys and lungs, leaving the stomach and intestines, and I boiled up another stew and ate it with more acorns. I was still hungry. Famished. There was no way a person could get fat living on such a diet. But you wouldn't starve, either, and some of the edge of my hunger was gone.

After that I looked at food, or game, very differently. With the onset of hunger in the woods – a hunger that did not leave me unless I killed something large, such as a deer, or killed and ate more than one rabbit or three or more grouse, or as many as ten or fifteen small fish – I never again thought simply in terms of steaks or choice portions of meat or vegetation.

As the hunger increases the diet widens. I have eaten grub worms wrapped in fresh dandelion greens. They were too squishy for me to want to chew them so I swallowed them whole, but I did eat

118

them and they stayed down. I have sucked the eyes out of fish that I caught the way Brian caught the panfish, with a homemade bow and willow arrows, sharpening the dry willow stalks and carving a shallow barb on the ends before fire-hardening them. I have also scaled fish with a spoon and then eaten the skin along with the cooked liver and brains. I ate rabbit brains too. I have eaten snake on survival courses, and it's surprisingly good. After reading a *National Geographic* about African natives when I was a boy, I tried eating both ants and grasshoppers. I found, as with the grub worms, they are easier to eat whole, wrapped in a leaf, although cooked grasshoppers are crunchy and, if you remember the salt, aren't bad – kind of like snack food.

Once the door was opened to eating strange food, or perhaps a better phrase might be odd aspects of familiar game and fish, I found I was ready for almost anything and that almost nothing would go to waste. This is not so astonishing really, when you consider that this practice was common among natives in most early cultures, and while much of it has been forgotten because of neglect and a bounty of cheap, readily available food, there are still sources for the knowledge.

When I was running my first Iditarod race I pulled into a village along the Bering Sea early in the day. This in itself was strange because for some reason I seemed to arrive at all the villages in the middle of the night. But it was early, before noon, and I'd run all night and was tired, as I thought the dogs were, but they suddenly took off at a dead run, passing the checkpoint where I was to sign in, barrelling down the village street until they came to a small dwelling where a little boy was kneeling over the carcass of a freshly killed seal. The dogs had smelled it, and it was only with the greatest difficulty that I finally got the snow hook buried in the packed snow and stopped them before they piled on top of the boy. I was terrified they might do him some injury – he was about six years old and small – but he seemed unconcerned and turned slowly when I pulled up. His mouth and chin were bloody and I could see that he had been sucking fresh blood out of a hole cut in the seal's neck. He smiled at me and gestured and said, "You want some?"

It was a generous offer and I didn't feel right rejecting it so I nodded and leaned down and tasted it. It was not unpleasant, although I would have preferred it cooked – as I'd eaten blood sausage, which I made by baking blood and flour in a bread pan – and I nodded and thanked him. Later I would see him walking down a passage between buildings eating straight lard out of a can with two fingers as if it were ice cream. Still friendly and courteous, he offered me a two-finger scoop of the white fat, but I thanked him and turned it down.

When I set out to write the *Hatchet* books I was concerned that everything that happened to Brian should be based on reality, or as near reality as fiction could be. I did not want him to do things that wouldn't or couldn't really happen in his situation. Consequently I decided to write only of things that had happened to me or things I purposely did to make certain they would work for Brian.

One of the hardest was to start a fire with a hatchet and a rock. I cast around for days near a lake in the north woods, searching for a rock that would give off sparks when struck with the dull edge of a hatchet. I spent more than four hours getting it to work. It seemed impossible. The sparks would fly and die before they hit tinder, or they would head off in the wrong direction, or not be hot enough, or some dampness in the tinder would keep it from taking. But at last, at long last, a spark hit just right and there was a tendril of smoke and then a glowing coal, and, with gentle blowing, a tiny flame, and then a fire. I can't think of many things, including the Iditarods or sailing the Pacific, that affected me as deeply as getting that fire going; I felt as early man must have felt when he discovered fire, and it was very strange but I didn't want to put it out. Even though I had plenty of matches and could easily start a new fire, there was something unique, something intense and important about this one campfire.

My one failure was eating a raw turtle egg. I finished *Hatchet* in the spring, while I was running dogs and training for my first Iditarod race. This was in northern Minnesota, not far from the Canadian border, in thick forest near hundreds of small lakes. It is one of the most beautiful places on earth and because of my heart trouble I can no longer take the winters up there, but I still miss it and remember my time there only with joy and wonder.

In the spring and early summer, after the snow is gone, you cannot run dogs on sleds, but there are old logging roads everywhere and you can have the dogs pull a light three-wheeled training cart. The dogs are very strong after a whole winter of training and racing and they view this as a kind of lark in which the object is to run as fast as possible down the old logging trails and to 'crack the whip' on corners and flip the cart into the ditch or the brush at the side of the road. I swear they laugh when they do this. And the driver's job is to keep the cart upright while running through the forest on the narrow old trails.

That spring I ran on some new trails that I hadn't used before, the snow had gone early and the ice was out. The topsoil up there is unbelievably thin. Though there is thick forest it is like the rainforest in South America: there is heavy growth because there is so much water, not because there is rich soil. On the logging roads the soil is gone and what remains is sand, as pure as any beach sand in the world. After all, in prehistoric times, the area was one large inland sea.

The sandy roads wind through countless lakes and still ponds in the woods and in each pond there are snapping turtles. Because I had not run these roads in the spring I didn't know that the female turtles come out to lay their eggs in the sand, and the best open sand they can find is on the logging roads.

These are big turtles, some of them two or more feet across. And they are ugly, and they are very, very mean. They always make me think of what you would get if you crossed a T-rex with an alligator. They hiss and snap and bite and can easily take a finger off. I once had a friend named Walter who got his rear end too close to a snapper on a river bank and I will always remember the sight of him running past me, naked, screaming, "Get it off! Get it off!" The snapper had locked, and I do mean *locked*, on to his right cheek and would not let go even when we finally stopped Walter and used a stick to try to pry the turtle's jaws apart. I suspect he still has a good scar there.

One day I came barrelling over a small hill around a corner thick with brush and the dogs ran directly over a female weighing about forty pounds in the process of laying eggs. Apparently she was not having a good day and we did nothing to improve her disposition. The dogs had never seen a turtle before and heaven only knows what they thought – probably that she was an alien sent down specifically to kill and eat dogs. Everything happened very fast. I saw her just as the dogs ran

124

over her, and she snapped at them left and right, hissing and spitting fur when she connected, and then the cart flipped on its side and the dogs left the trail and tried to climb the trees alongside the road and I rolled over the top of the snapper, screaming some words I thought I had forgotten as she took a silver-dollar-sized chunk out of my jacket, and the cart gouged a hole beneath her and dug up her eggs and we all tumbled to a stop.

I lay on my stomach, four feet beyond the turtle. The dogs were scattered through the trees, still in harness and tangled so badly that I would have to

use a knife to free some of them. For half a beat nothing moved or made a sound.

Then the turtle looked at the wreckage of her nest, the small round eggs scattered like dirty ping-pong balls; at me flopped there; at the dogs among the trees and the cart lying on its side, and she gave it all up as a bad try. With a final loud hiss, she dragged herself off the sandy trail and back to the swamp where she lived, looking very prehistoric and completely fed up.

As I began gathering up my pieces, my lead dog, Cookie – who was so smart and quick she never got tangled – reached around and deftly used her teeth to sever the tug holding her to the team (a habit I wished she would stop) and moved down to the turtle nest. She smelled one of the eggs, nuzzled it with her nose, then ate it whole. I knew skunks dug the nests up and ate them, because I had seen the torn-apart nests around lakes and swamps. Since I was writing *Hatchet*, it came to me that Brian would almost certainly run into a turtle nest, having crashed into a northern lake, and would be hungry enough to eat the eggs. I grabbed half a dozen of them before Cookie could eat them all. She let me have them without protesting, other than lifting her lip a bit – which should have been a warning to me that perhaps they were not as good as eggs might be – and I put them in the pocket of my jacket until I had a quiet moment.

Here we might look at several mistakes I made. First, I set myself too far away from the subject of my research: I had a full stomach; Brian was starving. Brian had just crashed in a plane; I had merely flipped over in a dog-training cart. And in the end Brian was desperate; I was only doing research.

With the dogs settled back into patched harnesses, I took out one of the eggs, cleaned the dirt off it, used my knife to cut the leathery shell slightly, and without waiting to think I tipped my head back and sucked out the contents.

I have eaten some strange things in my life: raw meat, eyeballs, guts. In the Philippines I tried to eat a local delicacy called a *baloot*, a duck egg with the baby duckling dead and fermented and half-rotten inside, and it all slithers out into your mouth with only a slimy lump here and there. I have eaten bugs, and I *know* that some of the food in army C rations was fermented road kill canned in lard and cigarette ash mixed with cat vomit.

But I couldn't hold the turtle egg down.

It hung halfway down my throat and tasted the

way I imagine Vaseline would taste if, somehow, it were rotten. I looked at the horizon and thought of wonderful things, of ice cream and steak and the apple pies my grandmother used to bake for me with light-brown crusts and sugar sprinkled on top, of lobster and cheeseburgers and vanilla malts, and I lost it.

I threw up turtle egg at terminal velocity, straight out like a runny yellow bullet, and Cookie, as if patiently waiting, licked it up, which made me throw up harder. She neatly caught the vomit before it could even hit the ground.

So it was the one bit of research I couldn't finish, though I tried three times. The second and third tries were worse, much worse, resulting in dry heaves and a snort from Cookie when nothing came. But I left it in because Brian was a different person, in a very different situation. Pushed to the limits of hunger he would probably have been able to keep the eggs down.

Even if they were slimy and yellow and tasted totally disgusting.

Rubbish

Andy Griffiths

It's Tuesday night

A very important night.

And not just because it's Valentine's Day, either.

It's rubbish-bin night.

And what's so important about rubbish-bin night?

Well, according to my mum and dad, the health of the entire neighbourhood depends on me remembering to put the rubbish-bin out.

Because if I forget to put the bin out, the garbage men can't empty the bin.

And if the garbage men can't empty the bin then we can't fit any more rubbish into it.

And if we can't fit any more rubbish into the bin then the rubbish will spill out over the top and on to the ground.

And if there's rubbish on the ground then the rats will come, and if the rats come, people will get sick, disease and pestilence will spread throughout the neighbourhood and everyone will die.

And, the worst thing is that I will get the blame. That's why rubbish-bin night is the most important night of the week: the fate of the neighbourhood is in my hands. Every man, woman and child is counting on me to remember to put the bin out.

And I haven't failed them yet.

I never forget.

Each week I tie a piece of white string around the little finger on my left hand to remind me.

The trouble is tonight I've tied it a bit too tightly and it's making my little finger throb. It's so tight that I can't get the knot undone. I'm going to have to cut it with a pair of scissors.

I go downstairs to the kitchen.

I pass Dad in the lounge room.

"Have you remembered what night this is?" he says.

"Yes, Dad," I say.

"Have you put the bin out yet?"

"Not yet," I say.

"Well, don't forget," he says. "I don't want

rubbish spilling out all over the ground. It will attract rats and . . ."

"I know, Dad," I sigh. "If the rats come people will get sick, disease and pestilence will spread throughout the neighbourhood and everyone will die."

"You think it's all a bit of a joke, do you?" he says, leaning forward in his chair and pointing his finger at me. "Well, we'll see how much of a joke it is when we're up to our ankles in rubbish and rats and you've got bubonic plague and you've got boils all over your body, funny-boy! And we'll all have a good laugh when bits of your lungs come flying out of your mouth and . . ."

"OK, Dad!" I say, "I get the picture! I'm going to put the bin out, all right?"

"Now?" he says.

"In a minute," I say. "Right after I cut this string off my finger."

"Don't forget," he says.

"I won't, Dad," I say. "I promise."

I swear my dad's getting crazier by the day.

I go into the kitchen, pull open the second drawer down and start rummaging for the scissors.

Mum comes into the room.

"Have you put the bin out?" she says.

"Not yet, Mum," I say. "I'm just about to."

"Well, don't forget," she says. "We don't want..."

"Rats," I say.

"How did you know I was going to say that?" she says.

"A lucky guess," I say.

The phone rings.

I go to pick it up.

"Don't touch that!" says Jen, pushing past me and beating me to the phone. "That'll be Craig. Besides, shouldn't you be putting the bin out? It stinks – I can smell it from my room."

"I'm surprised you can smell anything above your own stink," I say. Jen makes a face and picks up the phone.

I just keep standing there. She hates it when I listen in on her calls.

Jen puts her hand over the mouthpiece.

"Mum," she says, "Andy's listening to my call."

"I am not!" I say. "How can I be listening if you haven't even started talking?"

"You're *going* to listen," she says.

"Pardon?" I say.

"I said 'You're *going* to listen'," says Jen in a louder voice.

"What?" I say. "I can't hear you. I think I've gone deaf."

"Mum!" says Jen.

"Andy," sighs Mum, "you've got a job to do. Just go and do it."

"All right," I say, but I don't move. I just keep standing near the phone.

"Andy," says Jen.

"OK, OK!" I say. "I'm going!"

"That's not what I'm talking about," she says, holding the receiver towards me. "It's for you."

"For me?" I say.

"Yes," says Jen. "Hard to believe isn't it, but apparently someone wants to talk to you."

"Who?" I say. "Who is it?"

"Whom shall I say is calling?" Jen says into the phone.

She smirks.

"It's Lisa Mackney," she says.

"Lisa Mackney?" I say. "Are you sure?"

"Do you want me to ask her if she's sure she's Lisa Mackney?" she says.

"No!" I say, grabbing the receiver.

Lisa Mackney! Wow! She must have got my Valentine's card. I slipped it into her bag this morning. I wonder how she guessed it was from me.

133

Maybe the perfume on the envelope gave me away. Well, it wasn't exactly perfume. I couldn't find any, so I sprayed it with the pine-scented air freshener we use in the toilet. It went all over my clothes and I stunk of it all day. I guess she must have noticed.

Jen is still standing beside the phone.

"Mum!" I say. "Jen's listening to my call!"

"As if I'd want to listen to one of your juvenile phone calls," she says, walking out of the room. "I've *got* a life."

"Hello?" I say.

"Hi, Andy – it's Lisa," she says.

"Oh, um, er . . ." I stutter, trying to think of something clever to say. "Hi!"

"I hope you don't mind me calling you," she says.

Is she kidding? It's only the best thing that has ever happened in the history of the world. But I can't say this. She might think I'm making fun of her. I have to act cool.

"No," I say.

I can't think of anything else to say. Which is funny because I've got so much to say. I want to tell her how beautiful she is and how much I love her and how I wish she would be my girlfriend . . . but I can't find the words.

"You're not busy, are you?" she says. "I can call back later if you'd like."

What do I say to this?

If I say I'm not busy, she might think I'm some sort of loser with nothing better to do than just sit around the house. But if I say I am busy putting the bin out, she might think that I'm some sort of loser with nothing better to do than put the bin out.

I know honesty is supposed to be the best policy but in this case I think that dishonesty is even better.

"No, I'm just taking a breather," I say. "I've been doing a bit of weight-training . . . those five hundred kilogram weights can be pretty tough."

"You do weight-training?" she says.

"Oh, a little," I say.

"A little?" she says. "Five hundred kilograms is a lot!"

"Oh, not really," I say. "That's just a warm-up. It's the thousand kilogram weights that are really hard."

I hear Lisa gasp.

So far, so good. I think she's suitably impressed.

"Andy," she says, "can you be serious for a moment?"

"Huh?" I say. "I was being serious!"

Dishonest, but serious.

"I need to talk to you," she says. "It's important. I need to ask you a question. A serious question."

"OK," I say. "What is it?"

"Did you send me the card?"

"What card?" I say, playing dumb.

"The Valentine's card," she says.

"Oh, that card," I say, as casually as I can. "Yes, I did."

"I thought so!" she says.

There's an uncomfortable silence. I'm not sure what to say next.

"I wanted to thank you," she says.

"That's OK," I say.

"No, I meant in person," she says. "I was wondering if we could meet tomorrow morning? Before school?"

I can't believe it! She's practically asking me out on a date!

"Andy?" she says. "Are you there?"

No, I'm not here. I'm somewhere between the Earth and the moon I'm so happy. I have to try to come back. I have to answer her.

"Yes!" I say. "I'm here. Where would you like to meet?"

"How about outside the park near the school?" she says. "About 8.30?"

"OK, Lisa," I say. I'm keen to get off the phone now before I say anything stupid. "See you then."

"See you," she says. "And, Andy?"

"Yes?" I say.

"It wasn't a joke, was it?"

"What?" I say.

"The card?"

"No!" I say.

"Good," she says. "I'm really looking forward to it."

"Me too," I say. I want to add, "because you're beautiful and I love you", but I can't actually make the words because my mouth is just opening and closing like a fish's.

I hang up.

I can't believe it.

The most beautiful girl in the world just rang up and asked me out on a date. What if she asks me to go out with her? Can she do that? Can a girl ask a boy? I don't see why not. What if she asks me to marry her? Can we do that? Are we old enough? Will I need a ring? Or does the one who asks have to give the ring? What if she asks me to kiss her? I've never kissed a girl before. Not really. Not on

137

the lips. How do you do that? I'd better go and practise on my mirror.

I don't walk back up the stairs. I float.

Lisa rang me.

Lisa rang me and asked me out.

She asked me out.

I keep repeating it so that I can believe it.

Lisa rang me.

She asked me out.

I didn't ring her. She rang me. She must really like me after all. After everything bad that's happened.

I float into my room and flop on to my bed.

She loves me.

She loves me.

I lie on my bed and think about tomorrow morning.

I can see it now.

I'm walking up the road to the park. I have a dozen roses in my arms.

Lisa is standing there, looking beautiful.

Everything around her is sort of blurry, like in one of those romantic photos they have in the front of photographers' shops, but she is in the middle in perfect focus.

She smiles and waves.

138

"Hi, Lisa," I say, in a deep, strong and confident voice.

She looks into my eyes.

I look into hers. I feel like I'm melting.

"Hi," she says in a voice so soft and beautiful that she sounds like an angel.

I give her the roses.

"These are for you," I say.

She looks at the roses. Her eyes fill with tears.

"They're beautiful," she sobs. "Just beautiful . . ."

"Not as beautiful as you," I say, putting my arms round her.

I bury my face in her soft perfumed hair – every strand shining like it's spun from the finest gossamer.

"Oh, Andy," she says, "you are so thoughtful . . . so wonderful . . . so gentlemanly . . ."

"You forgot handsome," I say.

"And handsome," she says.

"And manly," I say.

"And manly," she says.

"And strong," I say.

"Be serious," she says.

"I was being serious," I say.

She stares at me.

"Before we go any further I have to ask you a question," she says.

"Anything," I say. "Ask me anything you want."

"Promise me you will answer truthfully, my darling," says Lisa.

"I promise," I say.

She leans forward and whispers into my ear.

Her breath sends shivers through my body that run right down into my toes. I feel dizzy and I hear a roaring sound as the blood rushes to my head. It's so loud I can hardly hear what she's saying. All I can hear is a roaring sort of grinding sound.

Lisa pulls away from me.

She's studying my face.

"Well?" she says.

"Well what?" I say.

"What's your answer?"

"What was the question?" I say.

"I said," she says, raising her voice above the roar, "did you remember to put the bin out?"

"The what out?" I say.

"The bin!" she screams.

The bin? The bin? What bin?

Oh no – the bin!!!

Suddenly the sun goes behind a cloud and the street around us is alive with rats – Lisa's hair turns to cobwebs, the skin peels off her face and she crumbles into a crumpled mummy-like heap on the footpath. I scream. The whole street dissolves – Lisa disappears. I open my eyes. The room's full of light. How could that be? I look across at the clock. It's 7.30 a.m. I must have fallen asleep! The room is full of the roar and grind of the rubbish truck out in the street. And my finger is throbbing. I forgot to cut the string off. But even worse – I forgot to put the bin out!

I jump off the bed and charge out of the room. Luckily I'm wearing my Action Man pyjamas. I can run faster when I'm wearing them. I leap down the stairs in one huge bound and spring for the back door.

I grab the bin. It's heavy – feels like it weighs at least a thousand kilograms – but luckily it's a wheelie bin. I tip it backwards and run as fast as I can with it down the drive – just in time to see the rubbish truck turn the corner at the bottom of the hill and disappear.

Aaggh!

Dad's going to kill me!

Mum's going to kill me!

If they don't die from the bubonic plague first, that is.

I have to get this bin emptied . . . and there's only one way to do it.

The rubbish truck can't be that far away. They have to stop all the time. And I'm a very fast runner when I need to be.

I take off down the hill.

Or rather the wheelie bin takes off down the hill and drags me along with it. If it wasn't for the stink this would be quite a fun ride. But at the bottom of the hill the ground levels out and I have to start pushing. I turn left up the next hill.

I can't do it!

It's too hard.

The bin is too heavy.

The hill is too steep.

Then I remember the rats.

I think of all the people in the neighbourhood who are going to die becuase I forgot to empty the bin. Little innocent children – still sleeping – oblivious of their fate. Oblivious of the fact that they are going to be deprived of life because I can't even remember a simple thing like putting the bin out on rubbish night. The fate of the neighbourhood depends on me. I have to go faster.

I bend over and put every bit of strength I have into pushing the bin up the hill. I'm going up at such an angle that the lid of the bin flips back and whacks me on the head. It's a blow that would have knocked anyone else out, but not me. I've got a very hard head. I flip the lid back and keep pushing. Nothing can stop me.

The roaring of the rubbish truck is louder now. I'm getting closer. I crest over the top of the hill and see it less than a hundred metres away.

"Stop!" I yell. "Stop! You forgot one!"

There are two men in fluorescent yellow vests running alongside the truck. They pick up the last two bins in the street and put them on the tray at the back. It lifts the bin up and empties the rubbish into the top of the truck.

I'm pushing the bin down the hill as fast as I can.

The men put the empty bins on to the side of the road and jump back on to the truck to ride to the next street.

"No!" I yell. "Please stop!"

One of them sees me coming and calls out to the driver.

The truck stops and I run up to it with my bin.

"Well, if it isn't Action Man!" says one of the men.

"You forgot this one," I say, panting hard. "From the next street."

"Forgot it?" he says. "That's not possible. Are you sure it was on the street when we went past?"

"Yes," I lie. This is another one of those situations where dishonesty is the best policy. It's a lie that could save many lives.

He looks at the other guy.

"Did you forget this one?"

"Nope," says the other one. "I would have seen it."

"Sorry, Action Man," says the first guy. "If it had been there we would have got it."

"Are you saying you don't believe me?" I say.

"I'm not saying anything, mate," he says. "I'm just saying we can't take it. If it's not outside the house then we're not permitted to empty it. For all I know you could be from out of our area – you could be trying to dump your rubbish illegally."

"But I'm not!" I say. "Why would I want to do that?"

"You'd be surprised what people try," he says, thumping the side of the truck. "OK, Mac!"

The truck takes off again and the man jumps up on the back.

I watch helplessly as the truck turns into the next street.

But I don't give up that easily.

I know a short cut through to the next street.

All I have to do is take the bin through, put it into position and hide. They'll empty it just like a regular bin.

I run down the hill a bit further and then turn right into a laneway. I push the bin for all I'm worth and within seconds I'm there.

Up in the distance I can see the yellow flashing lights of the truck. They've only just turned into the street. They're still too far away to see me.

Good.

I push the bin across the opening of the lane and head towards the nature strip, but the bin hits the gutter and lurches sideways.

I lose control and it hits the ground, spilling rubbish everywhere.

I can't believe what I'm seeing.

Half of the stuff from our garage is lying on the road. Mum and Dad must have had another cleanout. I hate it when they do that. They've thrown out some really good stuff. And some of it's mine. My old floaties. A house I made out of matchsticks. And my electric racing car set! I know the controls are missing, pieces of the track are broken and the cars have lost all their wheels, but that's no reason to throw out a perfectly good electric racing car set!

I'd better check there's nothing else of mine in there. I stand the bin up and look inside.

Oh no. I don't believe it!

She's chucked away the most valuable thing I own in the world – my faithful bath and shower companion – my rubber duck! I can see its little yellow beak peeking out from under the rubbish.

I look up.

The rubbish truck is about halfway along the street. I've got just enough time to get my duck and then scram.

"Don't worry!" I say. "I'll save you!"

I lean down into the bin, but I can't reach. It's right at the bottom.

I have to lean over further.

Uh-oh.

Too far!

I fall into the bin, headfirst into something squishy and smelly. It doesn't taste too good, either.

And what's worse, I can't move.

I can't get up.

The roaring of the truck is getting louder.

I kick my legs to try to make the bin fall over so I can wriggle out.

But my kicking is useless.

All it does is make the lid of the bin fall shut on top of me.

Now I'm trapped.

And nobody knows I'm in here!

The truck is right beside me. I can hear it. I feel the bin roll off the nature strip and land on the road with a bump. I think it's being put on the tray. I'm rising into the air. It's just like being in an elevator except much smellier.

I'm yelling my head off but it's no use. They can't hear me above the noise of the truck.

I clutch my duck. The bin tips upside down and we are dumped into the back of the truck with all the other rubbish.

The stink!

The stench!

The horror!

This has got to be the most disgusting thing that's ever happened to me.

I'm being churned around with all the rubbish. I try to scream but I get a mouthful of used tissues. Everything is a blur as bin after bin of fresh rotting rubbish is dumped on top of me. Mouldy vegetables, putrid fish and disposable nappies . . . I come face to face with a dead cat, but only for a moment – the churning just won't stop. Every time I catch my breath and work my way to the top of the pile a new bin-load knocks me down and the churning continues.

I've got to get out of here!

I've saved the neighbourhood, but I'm going to die!

I'll get bubonic plague.

I think I can feel it coming on already.

Dad's right.

There is nothing funny about being up to your knees in rubbish – and when it's over your head it's even unfunnier.

What a pity I won't live to tell him that.

Because I can't fight it any more.

I'm going to die, suffocated in rubbish.

I press my rubber duck to my chest, close my eyes and prepare for the end.

That's weird.

Everything has gone quiet.

The churning has stopped.

Maybe there's still hope.

I dig my way up out of the rubbish towards the light.

I push my head through a load of mouldy bread, empty dog food cans and used kitty litter.

But I don't care. I can see the sky!

I raise my duck above my head.

"We're going to make it," I say.

My duck quacks with joy.

I squirm and wriggle the rest of my body out from under the rubbish until I'm sitting on top of it all.

I wipe the slime from my eyes and look around.

We're travelling along a main road. The truck is obviously full and they're heading back to the tip to empty it. I've got to get out before that happens. I don't want to spend the rest of my life as landfill.

We pull up at a set of traffic lights.

This is my chance to escape.

I climb down over the back of the truck on to the platform, and just as the truck starts moving again, I jump clear. I hit the ground running, trip and roll into the gutter.

Ouch.

It hurts, but it's better than being in a rubbish truck any day.

"Are you all right?" says a voice.

A beautiful voice.

The voice of an angel.

I must be dead.

The bubonic plague got me after all and I've gone to Heaven.

But there's something familiar about that voice.

I open my eyes.

It's Lisa.

Lisa Mackney looking down at me.

"Andy?" she says.

"Lisa?" I say. "When did you die?"

"Die?" she says. "What are you talking about? We arranged to meet, remember?"

I sit up.

I look around.

This is not Heaven. This is Hell.

I'm outside the park.

Right where I said I would meet Lisa.

I'm right on time, but everything else is wrong.

As wrong as it possibly could be.

There she is looking clean and fresh and princess-like, her soft hair shining in the morning sun. And here am I, sitting in the gutter in my pyjamas covered in rubbish, surrounded by flies, clutching my rubber duck.

"I should have known you weren't serious," she says, pinching her nose and backing away from me. "I should have known it was all a joke."

"No, it wasn't!" I say, getting up and stepping towards her. A big slimy chunk of maggot-infested meat slides off my shoulder and plops on to the ground in front of her.

She puts her hand over her mouth and takes another step back.

"Keep away from me!" she says. "You . . . you . . . stink!"

I step towards her – kitty litter, cigarette butts and broken eggshells fall from my clothes and hair as I move.

She turns and runs.

I watch her. The girl I love. Running away from me in disgust.

What was supposed to be the best morning of my life has turned out to be the worst.

And the worst thing about it is that she's never going to want to kiss me now. All that practice on the mirror for nothing.

But at least I got the rubbish out. At least the neighbourhood is safe once more from the bubonic plague.

There's no telling how many lives I've saved.

Not to mention my rubber duck.

Perhaps all is not lost, after all.

I'm going to go home, cut this stupid string off my finger and have a long shower. A really long shower. I might even use some more of that air freshener – it was pretty strong. Then I'll go to school and explain everything to Lisa.

I'm sure she'll understand. In fact, I can see it now.

When she hears about what I've done, she'll realize what a hero I am. She'll apologize for saying that I stink. She'll beg me to forgive her. I will, of course. And then we'll kiss.

It's lucky I did all that practice on the mirror, after all.

ACKNOWLEDGEMENTS

The editor and publishers wish to thank the following for permission to use copyright material:

Joan Aiken: for 'Beezlebub's Baby' from *A Foot in the Grave* by Joan Aiken, first published by Jonathan Cape Ltd (1989). Copyright © 1989 Joan Aiken Enterprises Ltd, reproduced by permission of A M Heath & Co Ltd on behalf of the author.

Mary Arrigan: for 'Van Gogh's Potatoes' from *Screen,* first published by Poolpeg Press (1998). Copyright © 1998 Mary Arrigan, reproduced by permission of Ed Victor Ltd on behalf of the author.

Jon Blake: for 'The Tourists' from *The Likely Stories* by Jon Blake, first published by Viking (1991). Copyright © 1991 Jon Blake, reproduced by permission of Penguin Books Ltd.

Ruskin Bond: for 'The Monkeys' from *The Night Train at Deoli and Other Stories* by Ruskin Bond, first published by Penguin Books India Pvt Ltd, reproduced by permission of Penguin Books India Pvt Ltd and the author.

Joyce Dunbar: for material from *Software Superware* by Joyce and James Dunbar, first published by Macdonald & Co (Publishers) Ltd (1987). Copyright © 1987 Joyce Dunbar, reproduced by permission of Hodder and Stoughton Ltd.

Andy Griffiths: for 'Rubbish' from *Just Crazy!* by Andy Griffiths, first published by Pan Macmillan Australia (2000). Copyright © 2000 Andy Griffiths, reproduced by permission of Curtis Brown (Australia) Ltd on behalf of the author.

Paul Jennings: for 'Piddler on the Roof' from *Uncanny!* by Paul Jennings, first published by Penguin Books Australia (1988). Copyright © 1988 Paul Jennings, reproduced by permission of Penguin Books Australia Ltd.

Dick King-Smith: for 'Godfrey's Revenge' from *Ghostly Haunts*, compiled by Michael Morpurgo, first published by Pavilion Books Ltd (1994). Copyright © 1994 Fox Busters Ltd, reproduced by permission of A P Watt Ltd.

Gary Paulsen: for 'The Fine Art of Wilderness Nutrition' from *Hatchet: The Truth* by Gary Paulsen, first published by Random House Children's Books, a division of Random House Inc. (2001). Copyright © Gary Paulsen, reproduced by permission of Laurence Pollinger Ltd on behalf of the author.

ACKNOWLEDGEMENTS

Jamie Rix: for 'The New Nanny' and 'Glued to the Telly' from *Grizzly Tales for Gruesome Kids* by Jamie Rix, first published by Andre Deutsch Ltd (1990). Copyright © 1990 Jamie Rix, by permission of Scholastic Ltd.

Colin Thompson: for 'The Curse of Dogbreath Magroo' from *The Haunted Suitcase and Other Stories* by Colin Thompson, first published by Hodder Children's Books (1996). Copyright © 1996 Colin Thompson, reproduced by permission of Hodder and Stoughton Ltd.

Every effort has been made to trace the copyright holders but where this has not been possible or where any error has been made the publishers will be pleased to make the necessary arrangement at the first opportunity.